Real Mermaids
DON'T HOLD THEIR BREATH

HÉLÈNE BOUDREAU

sourcebooks
jabberwocky

Published by Sourcebooks Jabberwocky, an imprint of Sourcebooks, Inc.
P.O. Box 4410, Naperville, Illinois 60567-4410
(630) 961-3900
Fax: (630) 961-2168
www.jabberwockykids.com

Library of Congress Cataloging-in-Publication data is on file with the publisher.

Source of Production: Webcom, Toronto, Canada
Date of Production: March 2012
Run Number: 17325

Printed and bound in Canada.

WC 10 9 8 7 6 5 4 3 2 1

For Natalie, who always helps me keep it real

Chapter One

THE MONTH LEADING UP to my fourteenth birthday was the most exciting time of my life.

1. I found out my mom hadn't drowned but was actually a mermaid.
2. I discovered I was part mermaid too.
3. I rescued my mom from a bunch of mer-freaks in Talisman Lake and freed her into the ocean so she could have a chance to become human again.
4. I had my first kiss.
5. Did I mention my first kiss?

The month *since* my fourteenth birthday, however? Not so exciting.

My mom was *still* floating around in the ocean somewhere, and I had no idea if she'd ever make it back home. Plus, it was getting harder and harder to keep my mer-secret from my best friend Cori *and* I hadn't seen my crush Luke since he left for camp weeks earlier, so I was beginning to feel like I'd dreamt the whole first kiss thing up.

All in all, the month of July was beginning to feel like an Ice Age and a half—especially since I'd spent most of it scooping up ten trillion cones full of ice cream for every man, woman, and child in my small oceanside town of Port Toulouse.

I poked my head out from under the awning of Bridget's Ice Cream Parlor and glanced up and down Main Street, silently begging for Cori to come in early for her shift to save me from my suffering. The summertime ice cream "parlor" was basically a window of Bridget's Diner opening up onto the street. Customers could order from the sidewalk or come in and order from the counter.

"Hiya, Jade." My boss Bridget emerged from the kitchen and plunked a tub of ice cream into the cooler in front of me. "Got ya more Klondike Golden Vanilla."

"Thanks, Bridget." I managed a smile, thankful that she'd given me the job since I'd been bugging her to work there every year since I turned nine. I may have been having a cruddy summer so far, but the free ice cream samples were a definite perk.

"No problem, hon." Bridget adjusted the tub in line with the others inside the ice cream cooler. Just then, the bell over the front door jingled and a fresh crowd of hungry tourists and locals streamed into the diner, calling Bridget back to the main counter. "Gimme a holler if it gets busy."

"Okeydokey!" I answered.

But Bridget's Diner was always busy. Especially once summer was in full swing and Port Toulouse's population tripled in size, as boats sailed up our world-famous canal from the Atlantic Ocean to the "wild, rustic beauty of Talisman Lake." I scooped up a double order of cones and tried to ignore the crushing pain of frostbite shooting up my forearm while Chelse Becker collected the money and stashed it in our cashbox without counting it.

"Chelse," I whispered. "You still owe them thirty-seven cents."

But Chelse was in her own little world, bopping along to something thumping through her earbuds and staring at her cell phone. She'd recently come in second in KIX 96 Radio's Fastest Texter contest and seemed determined to take next year's title, judging by how fast her fingers were flying across her phone's screen.

"Enjoy your ice cream." I handed the customers their change after nabbing it from the cashbox.

Chelse's family had a cottage across the lake from my Gran's in Dundee. You might wonder how a girl like private-schooled, country-clubbed, equestrian-trained Chelse came to work at Bridget's instead of spending her summer jet-skiing or working on her tan (I know I did). Turns out, Chelse's sixteen with a car and can do drop-offs and pick-ups for the restaurant in a pinch—plus, she was in a bit of a financial bind.

"And *then*," Chelse had complained, three weeks before,

as she dumped her bag next to the counter on our first day of Ice Cream Parlor duty, "my mom said I couldn't bring friends to the cottage until I paid for the canoe. It wasn't *my* fault it drifted off and I missed curfew. That idiot ex-boyfriend of mine must have tied it up wrong."

Oops.

Chelse would trample me with her prize-winning show horse if she ever found out I was to blame for losing her canoe. Not like I planned to tell her that I'd borrowed it to transport my mermaid mother to the freedom of the ocean, but I couldn't let her take the fall either.

So, with every scoop I scooped, I mentally watched my paycheck go into the Pay Back the Beckers for their Rare Aboriginal Canoe Fund instead of saving up for that new laptop I'd been drooling over. I hadn't exactly worked out *how* I was going to pay Chelse back without blowing my cover but until then, I'd tucked the money away and made do with my ancient laptop's missing L key. One, so I could relieve my guilty conscience, and two, so Chelse could quit her job and Bridget could hire someone who actually knew how to make change and didn't need seventeen phone apps to get through her day.

"Hey, Sunshine." Cori finally arrived, wearing an awesome *Cori Original* denim sundress and hand-dyed cotton scarf. "Look who finally decided to make an appearance." She rolled her eyes and tilted her head out into the diner.

Trey. And Luke. First-kiss Luke.

"Lu—" I tried to wave but Cori caught my arm and

pulled it down. She gave me a wide-eyed-pursed-lips-shake-of-the-head look before disappearing into the kitchen to stash her stuff.

From what I could tell, Luke hadn't seen me across the crowded, noisy diner. He stood with his back to me as he waited with his brother for a booth to clear out.

"I'm not sure if they have gelato, honey." A woman stood at the parlor window with her little boy, thankfully interrupting me from making a total idiot of myself. She patted a fussy, brand new baby in a sling and tried to contain the struggling toddler with her free hand. "Just give me a second while I get Olivia settled and I'll ask the girl."

"Huh?" I asked, blinking uncontrollably. It took me a minute to catch on to what the customer was saying. I recognized the mom from Dooley's Pharmacy a couple weeks before, only now she had an extra baby to go along with her rubber band of a toddler. She looked like she hadn't slept in days. "No, sorry, we don't serve gelato. All our stuff's made from local dairy products." I smiled at the toddler and tried to catch his eye to distract him. "Made with *real* cows."

The boy laughed and stopped pulling on his mother's arm.

"Did you know," I continued, trying to distract him long enough for his mom to readjust the binkie in her baby's mouth, "we get our chocolate ice cream from *brown* cows, vanilla from the *white* cows, and strawberry from cows that forget to put on sunscreen?"

The boy put a hand over his mouth to stifle a giggle

and jumped up and down. I leaned over the counter and tousled his hair then turned to his mom.

"I'm pretty sure they serve gelato bars at Mug Glug's across the street." I pointed to Mug Glug's awning.

"Thanks." She smiled appreciatively and took the boy's hand to turn to go.

I waved as they left then glanced across the diner.

Cori reemerged from the kitchen and slapped my arm with her apron before pulling it over her head. "Don't you *dare* go over there. You've lasted this long. Don't cave now."

I turned to see that Luke and Trey were now sitting in their usual booth by the window. I say "usual" but I hadn't seen Luke there since he left for Outward Bound at Camp Whycocomagh at the beginning of the month.

"You're right. I know you're right." I peeled a banana and got started on that morning's sixth banana split.

"Of course I'm right." Cori replenished the stack of waffle cones. "Not a phone call, not a text for the whole entire time he was gone. Unacceptable."

"Yeah, but the camp *does* have a no cell phone policy," I pointed out. "At least that's what their website says. Remember that for when Trey goes in August." Luke and Trey took turns at the camp and traded off mowing lawns during the rest of the summer.

"Seriously, Jade?" Cori looked up from her pile of cones and sighed in exasperation. "You checked the website?"

"What?" I dolloped strawberry sauce over the banana split. "It's up there for everybody to see!" I was just taking a page from Dad's book and using technology for the power of good.

"And has Luke called since he got back from camp? Nooo." Cori stretched out the word and sneered. "Those Martin boys are all the same. Trey hasn't called me since Sunday either." She stopped piling cones and eyed me seriously. "You haven't broken down and called *Luke*, have you?"

"No."

"Texted him?"

"No."

"Creeped his Facebook page?"

"Nn-oo." I hoped Cori didn't detect the hesitation in my voice over the *schkrrrr* sound of the aerosol whipped cream.

"Good girl. Because, trust me," Cori warned, "if you text him first, you've pretty much given up any relationship power you may have possessed up until that point."

I had a feeling Cori had read one too many *Teen Cosmo* magazines but I'd listened to her. And I'd suffered in silence. And I certainly didn't scribble Luke's name on every piece of scrap paper lying around the house or practice what I'd write in his yearbook. And I definitely didn't do every compatibility quiz in my own *Teen Cosmo* magazines just to find out whether our summer romance was "Made in the Shade," "Too Hot to Handle," or "Too Cool for School."

Nope, not me.

But Cori was right; except for a couple texts before he left for camp, Luke had basically ignored me since her pool party—which isn't so unusual, given my dating history.

But Luke was a mer. Like me. Didn't that count for something?

"Uh…I think that's good." My customer, Mr. Howser, nodded at the mound of peanuts I'd piled onto his banana split.

His wife got two spoons from the spoon cup and looked at me skeptically. "Are you okay, dear?" she asked.

"Oh! Yeah, okay. Sorry!" I smiled, but the more I thought about the Luke situation, the more irked I got.

I stole another glance at the Martin brothers' booth while I squirted a final squiggle of chocolate sauce over the banana split. Who did Luke think he was, anyway?

I served up the banana split then pulled off my apron.

"I'm taking my break."

Cori caught my arm and stared me down. "Why do I get the feeling you're about to flush three weeks of self-control down the toilet?"

"Don't worry. I'm doing this for all of womankind. Guys have been getting away with this stuff for far too long."

"This can only end badly." Cori dropped her hand from my arm and joined Chelse at the ice cream cooler.

I ignored her and stalked around the counter and across the diner in ten long strides. Luke was going to live to regret dissing me. He looked up when my right foot came down hard onto the clickety tile floor like a soldier on march.

"Well, well, well…look who just decided to *resurface*," I said, silently pleased with my ironic choice of words. I was on *fire*.

"Hey, Ja—"

"Save it." I put a hand up to stop him.

Both he and Trey gulped. Good. I had them right where I wanted. Intimidated and off balance. I was going in for the kill.

"Not that I give a flying flip phone what has been going on with you for the past three weeks, but FYI: kissing a girl, then basically going all radio-silent on her is *not* cool. So, unless you're about to tell me you've been roaming the plains of Africa on the hunt for the last wildebeest with no visible signs of civilization for ten thousand miles, I don't want to hear your excuse."

Score.

That rolled off my tongue *way* too easily. I gave myself a mental pat on the back, crossed my arms, and waited for whatever weak, pathetic excuse he had to offer.

Luke shifted in his seat and winced. He looked at Trey before turning back to me.

"I'm, uh…I'm really sorry, Jade," he said quietly. "I was gonna give you a call as soon as I got home from camp but our mom was rushed to the hospital in Renworth on Sunday. We just brought her back home today."

Oops?

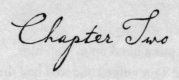

Chapter Two

I MANAGED TO MAKE MY way back to the scooping station without tripping over my jaw, but barely.

The rest of my conversation with Luke had gone something like this.

"Gah. Mrumpt. Uh…me. Oh, well then. Urp." And that's when Luke got a call that the new blade for his lawn mower had come in at Harry's Hardware Store and he had to go.

How could I have been so stupid? Here I was, ready to rip the poor guy's head off, and all the while he'd been at his mother's bedside at the *hospital*.

Cori, the scooping goddess, had weeded the line of customers down to nothing by the time I got back. She shut the cooler lid to keep the chill in, then turned and leaned against it with her arms crossed and her mouth set in a thin line. Chelse was cracking open rolls of pennies while peering at the screen of her phone, unaware of the violent mer-micide about to happen right beside her.

I held an arm across my face. "Sorry, sorry! Please don't hurt me, I just couldn't help myself."

"Didn't I tell you? Didn't I *tell* you?!" Cori held out her arms and gave me a quick hug.

"Ugh. Now I feel like a total jerk."

"Spill. What happened?" Cori picked up a washcloth and wiped the ice cream stickiness from her hands.

"Well, mystery solved. They weren't being idiots and ignoring us." I hunted for the bag of peanuts under the counter to restock our peanut bin. "They were actually three hours away at Renworth Hospital with their mom."

"They were?" Cori's face softened. She turned to glance across the diner to catch a look at Trey and gasped when she realized he'd been waiting for her on the other side of the counter, just a few feet away. Trey held out a small bouquet of wild daisies like the kind that grew near the bridge.

"There might be a few bugs in them. Sorry?" Trey smiled and raised his eyebrows in an expectant expression. Geesh, those Martin boys sure knew how to turn on the charm. And from the look on Cori's face, she was totally going for it hook, line, and sinker.

"Trey!" Cori grasped the bouquet in one hand and leaned over the counter to give him a peck on the cheek.

"Sorry. Things have been really crazy," Trey said.

"What happened? When you didn't call I was *so worried*!" Cori caught my eye and gave me a buggy-eyed "work with me" look then turned back to Trey. "How's your mom?"

Trey slid onto a counter stool and pulled Cori's hand into his. "Her epilepsy has been a bit worse than usual. We took her to Urgent Care here in town but the seizures got really bad on Sunday night, so they rushed her to Renworth Hospital. We hardly had time to pack a bag."

"Is she okay?" I realized I hadn't even asked Luke that before he had to go.

Trey's face was somber. "It took them a while to get the seizures under control." He turned to Cori. "I really wanted to call but we were staying at my uncle's summer trailer nearby and between the no-Internet zone at the trailer park and—"

"No cell phones in the hospital," Cori finished for him. Her mom was a nurse at the cottage hospital nearby so she got it.

"Yeah. So…" Trey fiddled with a strand of Cori's hair and smiled. "Am I in the doghouse?"

"Of course not!" Cori swooned. "But is your mom okay now?"

"Yes." Trey let out a breath of relief. "She's pretty wiped but at least she's home."

I let out a breath too, not realizing I'd been holding it in. "I'm really glad she's okay."

"Thanks, Jade." Trey gave me a friendly smile and went back to gazing into Cori's eyes.

Customers were starting to gather at the takeout window again, so I gave my hands a quick wash and got back to work, thankful for the distraction. Of course, I was happy Cori and Trey had worked things out, but with my awkward conversation with Luke still fresh in my mind, I wasn't really in the right head space to watch their happy reunion.

Three double-scoop sugar cones and a strawberry sundae later, Cori breezed back to the cooler with a goofy grin.

"All good?" I asked with a smile. And yes, it was sincere. Cori was my girl; it was nice to see her happy.

"More than good." Cori rubbed the goose bumps from her forearm. "He's picking me up later and we're going roller-blading along the boardwalk by the beach. Hey, why don't you and Luke come too?"

Trey had obviously forgotten about the verbal diarrhea I'd spewed earlier.

"Yeah, I'm not really sure if the Luke-and-me thing is still happening," I said quietly.

Before Cori could answer, Chelse's stool scraped along the floor as she stood from her perch at the cashbox. She checked the time on her cellphone.

"Shift's over. I'm out." Her voice cracked when she spoke. I wasn't sure if it was because of the underuse of her vocal chords, since she hadn't actually said more than ten words to me throughout our whole shift, or whether she was upset.

"You okay?" I searched her face.

Then, the impossible happened. Chelse forced a smile and *turned off her phone.* As in, cut off her main source of communication with the outside world. Her screen went blank as her phone powered off. She tucked it in her bag and got her sweater from the back of her stool.

"Yeah. I'm good, thanks." She signed off on the time sheet attached to the clipboard by the soft-serve machine then disappeared through the kitchen to the back door.

"What the heck was *that* all about?" I asked, washing my hands so I could take over cash box duty while Cori got to work at the cooler.

"Probably something about her ex-boyfriend. It looked like she was on his Facebook profile earlier. But wait a sec." Cori plopped a scoopful of Mooseprint Mocha into a paper cup and handed it over to a touristy-looking elderly woman then turned and whispered to me. "What's this about you and Luke?"

I made change for the lady and complimented her on her flowery hat, then asked if she needed another napkin and suggested some Port Toulouse landmarks she might want to explore on her trip. Cori poked me in stomach with her elbow. I smiled at the lady and bid her good-bye before Cori cracked one of my ribs.

"I just kind of went off on him," I admitted. Sure I was ticked about him not calling me since we kissed, but it was more than that. Luke was the only other person I knew like me—a mer. Other than Mom, that was. But Mom wasn't there just then and Luke was. Thinking I'd screwed up that mer-to-mer connection made me feel more lost than ever. Not that I could admit that to Cori. "Roller-blading with me is probably the last thing on Luke's priority list."

"Aw, Jade. I'm sure it's not so bad. Why don't I get Trey to talk to him?"

But I couldn't do that. It wasn't like we were in fourth grade and could get away with passing notes to each other with check boxes to find out:

Do you like me?

☐ Yes

☐ No

"Nah…I think it's just best if I cut my losses." I didn't need *Teen Cosmo* to tell me that our summer romance had probably come to its thrilling conclusion.

That's when a busload of day-campers and their counselors converged on us, shutting down our conversation, which was just as well.

I'd been so focused on Luke that I hadn't given enough of my brain space to the other mer in my life. Mom was stuck in the ocean, waiting for the Mermish Council to decide when she could become human again. Or was she in the magical tidal pool undergoing her transformation already? Gah! I needed to find out what was going on with Mom or I'd drive myself crazy wondering. Crazier than usual, anyway.

From then on, I vowed to put Luke Martin out of my mind and turn my attention to bringing Mom home. I was sure that was exactly what I needed to get my head on straight again.

Forget boys, especially adorable mer-boys like Luke Martin.

I had bigger fish to fry.

Chapter Three

"DID I JUST HEAR you correctly?" Dad called from underneath the bathroom sink as he attempted to replace the faucet. I could hear the smile in his voice.

"What?" All I had said was I thought we could use a plumber.

CLANG, DING, CLANG.

"We don't need a plumber." Dad's pudgy legs poked out from underneath the sink as he worked to get comfortable. "I just didn't realize there was an up and a down on this valve thing. No biggie, I'll figure it out."

I scrolled through my Google search for local plumbers on Dad's iPad. AAA Drain Repair all the way through to Zooter Rooter Plumbing Services. At least *they* would know which direction to install a bathroom faucet.

"All I'm saying is there are professionals who depend on this kind of work to feed their families, you know."

I wasn't sure if Dad's latest do-it-yourself kick was to make the house look nice for when Mom finally got home or whether he was just trying to distract himself while he waited. There was the new paint job in the living room, some project he and Luke's grandpa Eddie were working on in the garage, and now the plumbing job to replace the leaky faucet. Oh, and the plugged bathtub drain would probably need to be addressed at some point.

"Sheesh, have a little faith!" Dad called over the clanging. "I'm an engineer, after all. How hard can it be to change a bathroom faucet?"

I leaned over and hollered into the sink.

"Apparently, harder than quantum physics!" My voice bellowed down the drainpipe. The sound made him jump.

"Hey!" A hand appeared from below and a crumpled wad of packing tape sailed toward me. It missed me by a mile.

"Ouch, I'm hit!" I faked a cry. "This is definitely going to need stitches."

"Yeah right!" Dad's hand disappeared again. More clanging noises.

"Hey, is the main water valve still off?" I called down, trying to figure out the instructions on the sheet of paper that had come with the faucet.

"Give me a little credit, Jade. They teach that kind of thing in engineering school too, you know." Dad popped his head up from under the sink and stood to survey his handiwork. "There! All done. See? That didn't take any time at all."

I checked my watch. "Yep. Only three hours and forty minutes, seven Google searches, and two trips to Home Depot. Record time."

The cell phone rang. We both froze and stared at it vibrating on the vanity's countertop, just like every other time the phone had rung in the past three weeks. Was it Mom? Was she safe?

I picked it up on the second ring. "Hello?" I asked hopefully.

"Congratulations! You've been selected for an exclusive three-day Frontier Alaskan Cruise…"

I clicked off the phone and tossed it back on the counter. "Argh! Another telemarketer. Seriously, do people actually fall for that stuff?"

Dad let out a breath, then turned to clean up the extra parts and packaging from the faucet box. But I could see his expression in the bathroom mirror. His face was flushed red and his eyes shone with disappointment. Crushing, heartbreaking disappointment.

"Dad?"

"Yeah?" He cleared his throat and looked up in the mirror, meeting my gaze, then busied himself arranging tools into his metal toolbox. The sound reverberated through the hollowness of the bathroom.

"I want to go to the ocean to go see what's happening with Mom." The last time I'd seen Mom was underneath the pier at the Descousse Marina. Sure, she'd said the Mermish Council was going to let her use the tidal pool so she could transform into a human again, but what if something had gone wrong? And why was it taking so long?

Dad shut the toolbox's lid. It snapped shut on his finger.

"Oh! Ouch." He snatched his hand back and sucked on his finger. "Yeah, sure, honey. We've been up and down the coast looking for the tidal pool already, but maybe we can look around Gros Nez Point this time."

This wasn't going to be easy. How was I going to convince Dad that I didn't want to do just another one of our evening coastal hunts up and down the shores around Port Toulouse? I wanted to go straight to the source. I wanted answers. Real answers. And there was only one place to get them.

"No, Dad. The ocean…the actual ocean."

"Oh, honey. No—"

"Please? Not knowing what the heck is happening with Mom is making us both a little batty. We can't jump each time the phone rings. And honestly," I stared at the loose wires hanging from the half-installed bathroom fan overhead, "I'm not sure how many more home improvement projects we can survive before one of us gets electrocuted."

Dad blinked a few times.

"No." He picked up the toolbox and brushed by me. I sighed and followed him out the door and down the stairs. Dad kept ignoring me through the rec room door and out into the garage, but I pressed on.

"Wouldn't you love to know what's going on? To have some idea when Mom was actually coming home? Whether she was coming home at all?"

Dad stood squarely in front of his workbench. He ran

his hands along the lid of the toolbox before turning to me. "Of course I want to know, Jade. But I've already almost lost one Baxter girl to the ocean. I really don't feel like risking another."

"I promise I'll be careful," I pleaded.

"It's not like you're asking me to go to the movies by yourself, Jade. What you're proposing is extremely dangerous. There are tidal forces, salinity and buoyancy factors to consider…"

Great. Dad was totally geeking out on me.

"Plus," he continued, "the Atlantic is not like Talisman Lake, where you can just turn in any direction and find your way back to shore. This is the ocean, Jade. One wrong turn and next stop is the British Isles." He patted the pockets of his pants and looked around the garage as if he'd misplaced something, then peeked under a tarp covering our old camping trailer—except it wasn't exactly our camping trailer anymore.

"What did you do to the trailer?" I asked pulling off the rest of the tarp. "What is this thing?"

Dad cringed as though I'd found my presents a week before Christmas. "Uh, just something Eddie and I have been tinkering with."

The trailer's canvas top had been removed, and an old hot tub took up most of the floor space inside. Hoses and pipes came off the hot tub at all angles, and a tangle of wires was connected to a laptop on the counter at the far side of the trailer.

"Well, I guess this is as good a time as any to show you." Dad climbed the steps into the trailer and held out his hand to help me up. He squeezed his way around the tub, which was filled with water, and took a seat in front of the laptop. The laptop flashed on and Dad opened a program with graphs and data. He pressed a button to start the hot tub jets, sending bubbles whirring through the water.

"When did you have time to do all this?" I asked, amazed.

"Eddie, or rather Dr. Schroemenger," Dad said, reminding me of when we'd found out Eddie was actually a mer expert who had published an article about a mer discovery when he was a university professor in Florida—Eddie was laughed at and lost his job over it, so now he preferred to keep his mer discoveries to himself— "amassed a lot of information from his years of research. He analyzed the water-to-air ratio of hundreds of tidal pools and found them fairly constant. Our theory is that the tidal pool the Mermish Council uses to transform mers to humans isn't magical at all. And in fact, Eddie's contact in Florida has found the same thing."

"You mean the Mermish Council just made that up? To keep other mers from trying it on their own?"

"Well not many mers know about the possibility of becoming human, so they wouldn't give tidal pools a second glance. It actually all comes down to sound scientific principals of accelerated evolution and devolution. I just applied Eddie's data to an algorithm and we came up with this."

"Okay, okay." I held my head and watched air rush through the jets. "Assume I didn't understand a word you just said. What exactly is *this*?"

"The Merlin 3000." Dad beamed.

"What does the 3000 stand for?" I asked.

"Nothing, it just sounds cool." Dad smiled and fiddled with one of the knobs on the hot tub.

"But what, exactly, does the Merlin 3000 *do*?" I felt a spark of hope growing in my chest.

"It's a mer-to-human synthesizer equipped with what we believe are the correct ratios of air and water, fully optimized with salinity sensors and temperature gradients. And it's portable." Dad slapped the side of the trailer and smiled.

"Like a fake tidal pool? To changes mers to humans?" I cried. "So, this is it! This is how we can get Mom back!"

"No, now wait, Jade. The Merlin 3000 is still in its proto-type stage. There are still a lot of variables we don't know yet." Dad powered off the computer and turned off the jets. Bubbles traveled to the surface of the water and popped as the air pump whirred to a stop. "We just thought it would be a good idea to work on a backup plan just in case."

Dad stepped down the stairs and waited for me to do the same before he pulled the tarp back over the trailer.

"But what if Mom never made it to the tidal pool? What if she's trying to figure out how to get back to us? If we could find her, we could test this thing out. Let me go find her, Dad. Please?"

"No. Absolutely, unequivocally no. Sorry, Jade."

I followed Dad back into the house and up to the bathroom.

"But," I got the wastepaper basket and started filling it with bubble wrap, "I just can't go through the rest of the summer without knowing. Can you?"

Dad looked up at the ceiling and let out a long breath.

"Okay, okay," he finally said. "I have to admit I'm having a hard time with the wait too."

My heart leapt. "So you'll let me go?"

He eyed me seriously and took forever to reply. "Only if we do it my way, okay?"

"Yes. Yes! Whatever you want." I jumped up and down and gave Dad a hug. He laughed and shook his head.

"I'll get Eddie to take us in the Martins' boat on Saturday. It's got a depth sounder and a fish finder and is equipped with state-of-the-art nautical charts and electronic weather tracking. I need this to be as safe as possible, got it?"

"Saturday's good. It's my day off and I was thinking Saturday anyway. Yes, Saturday! You're the best. Thanks. You won't regret this! Really!" I kept tidying up the bathroom to prove my enthusiasm. Something sparkly caught my eye amid the extra washers and leftover faucet parts. I picked it up and examined it.

My toe ring.

"You found it," I whispered.

"Yeah, it came up when I snaked the drain, trying to unplug it. It must have fallen in that time..." He didn't have to finish—that time my toes and feet and legs turned into a tail for the first time.

"Wow, everything changed after that, huh?" I twirled the toe ring between my fingers and rubbed off a piece of gunk wedged between the grooves.

"That's for sure." Dad took the toe ring from me and inspected it with a smile. "The tub has never drained quite the same way since."

"Ha ha." I snatched the toe ring back from him and started to turn on the faucet to wash it off but hesitated. "Is it safe to turn this thing on?"

"Of course! Should be good as new."

I turned on the faucet and held my breath. Water flowed from the spout. Miracles did happen!

"See, I told you I knew what I was doing." Dad smiled and shook his head. "And you thought we should call a plumber."

Just then, I felt a drip on my toe.

"Uh, Dad?"

"Yes?" He replaced the soldering gun in its case.

Drip. Drip.

"Wasn't that conference you went to in June about fluid dynamics or something?"

"Mm-hmm…why?"

Then a trickle.

"Well, I think that's going to come in handy." I opened the doors underneath the sink. Water gushed out all over the floor.

"Ah!" Dad cranked off the tap.

I pulled a beach towel from the rack and caught the puddle before it turned into a tidal wave. We slipped and slid on the bathroom tile, trying to sop up the mess.

"Should I make the call?" I blew a curl from my forehead.

"Make the call." Dad squeezed water from the bath mat into the bathtub.

I reached for the phone and dialed one of the numbers from my Google search.

"Hello! Mr. Zooter? Yeah, we've got a problem!"

Chapter Four

I SKIPPETY-SKIPPED TO BRIDGET'S THE next day, scooped a bunch of ice cream, and didn't even mind working my whole shift with Chelse as she carried on with her texting drama. Apparently, her cell phone break was over and a few glances at her screen revealed that the carnage had indeed spread over to Facebook. Was no virtual place safe from the frenzied fingers of Chelse Becker?

Friday afternoon lunch rush was finally over. I just had to get through a few more hours of scooping duty and then the next day's Mer-to-Mom Rescue Mission planning could begin. Finally, some answers!

I took advantage of the slow down in customers and scarfed down an order of Bridget's cheesy nachos with extra jalapenos and washed it down with a bowlful of Wig Wag Wigout, my own special creation of Nutter Butterscotch Ripple ice cream with Wigwag chocolates crumbled on top.

I was in my happy place.

"Rumor has it that all your ice cream is made with real cows."

My stomach did a somersault as I looked up and saw who it was. Luke held the Holstein cow tip jar from the counter up to his face, trying to match its cow-like expression. He set it back down and it toppled over, sending the cover rolling across the countertop. I scrambled to help him catch it, and our hands brushed against each other. My face felt hot and I wondered if the moment could be any cheesier. It was like a scene from a chick flick, except I felt like I was playing the part of the awkward best friend instead of the charming love interest.

"Luke…" I stole a glance at Chelse to see if she could bail me out and serve him while I faked a trip to the bathroom. I couldn't talk to Luke! Not without rehearsing every itty-bitty detail in my head to avoid making an idiot of myself like I had the day before.

Chelse looked my way and rolled her eyes. My real-life troubles obviously paled in comparison to her virtual ones. I flashed her a thanks-for-nothing eye bulge and turned back to the takeout window to face Luke.

I was on my own.

"If you're looking for suggestions, I just had the Nutter Butterscotch and it is delicious. I recommend a crumbled Wigwag topping. My specialty." I tried to keep my tone as businesslike as possible, but I was sure I sounded like my brains had been scooped out and put through a salad spinner.

Luke braced his hands on the counter and looked over the cooler lid to scan our selection. "As good as they all look, I'm not really here for the ice cream."

"Oh. Well, you can get frozen yogurt at Mug Glug's," I offered. What was *wrong* with me? I owed the guy an apology, big time, and all I could do was blow him off with dairy-related chitchat.

"Cori says you get off your shift soon," Luke said.

"Um, no…actually I work until five." I made a mental note to kill Cori.

"Actually, she's off right now." I felt someone yank the dish towel from my shoulder and flick the back of my leg. Speak of the devil.

"Ouch. And you're early," I whispered to Cori, turning toward her.

"And *you're* welcome," she whispered back. She looked up at Luke and smiled. "Jade will meet you in the parking lot out back in a couple minutes."

"Got it." Luke drummed his fingers on the counter, then gave an adorable salute before disappearing past the ice cream parlor window.

I turned and grabbed the towel back from Cori. "What are you trying to do to me? What am I supposed to say to him?"

"How about 'I'm sorry' closely followed by 'How's your mom?' and then finish it off with a 'That Cori is *so* awesome, isn't she?'"

"Ha ha." I folded the dish towel until it was an itty-bitty square then shook it open again and tossed it on the counter.

"Seriously, Jade—you can do this." Cori unhooked the time sheet clipboard from its nail and handed it to me.

"Weren't you the one who told me to stay away from

the Martin boys?" I took the clipboard from her. "Are you saying you weren't right, after all?"

"Yeah, well…it's not that I'm always *right*, I'm just never wrong. So, step away from the ice cream cooler. You are being relieved of your duties."

I looked at her with an exasperated smile.

"All right, all right." I found my name on the time sheet and signed out. "I might as well apologize so I can breathe my last breath with a clear conscience before I die of embarrassment."

"Good girl." Cori held out her hand for the clipboard but Chelse took it from me before I could hand it over.

"A friendly word of advice?" Chelse signed out for her break and shoved the clipboard back onto its nail. She tossed her cell phone into her purse and swept by me. "Guys suck."

"Wow," I whispered to Cori once Chelse was out of earshot. "That was weird."

Cori pulled down the lever to fill a sugar cone with swirls of soft-serve vanilla. "Yeah, well, not sure if you've been on Facebook lately but there's a really embarrassing video of Chelse being posted and shared. I'll admit I snuck a peek. It's kind of cringe-worthy."

"Really?" I glanced over as Chelse pushed through the diner door. I knew it was probably wrong, but I was dying to know. "What's the video of?"

"Just something stupid. I'll tell you more about it later, but go. Luke's waiting for you, remember?"

Remember? I pictured Luke making that adorably

silly cow face and sighed. Luke Martin was kinda hard to forget.

Luke was sitting on the curb of the back parking lot when I came out of the kitchen door. He stood when he saw me and slid his hands deep into the pockets of his cargo shorts.

I felt for the toe ring I had strung on a chain around my neck. It brought me back to that night in the tub, the first time I'd ever changed from feet to flippers. The weirdness between Luke and me would be a big bummer, since I really wanted to talk to him about this whole mer thing. Who else could understand what it was like to be me?

Luke looked like he was debating what to say, judging by the way his eyebrows scrunched together and the slow breath he was exhaling. What if this was the final showdown? What if I didn't get a chance to apologize before he dumped me for good?

"Luke, I…" I began, but the rest of the words got stuck in my throat like a dry cracker.

Luke held out his hand for me.

"Walk?" he asked, nodding to the path that followed the canal to the beach.

I nodded and took his hand.

Luke's hand. In mine. What did this mean?

We walked along the mile-long canal that separated the Atlantic Ocean from the fresh water of Talisman Lake. Luke's grandpa, Eddie, was in charge of opening and closing the canal's lock when boats wanted to sail through. But the canal's lock served another purpose. The Mermish Council used Talisman Lake as a prison and the lock kept the criminal mers, "Freshies," from escaping.

"You totally knew I was down there that day, didn't you?" I remembered how Luke had looked into the water the day I finally got Mom and Serena through the locks to the ocean.

"I almost dove in when I saw you were down there, but I figured that would blow your cover."

"Thanks for nothing. I was freaking out down there!" I slapped his arm as we continued walking. "So, I still don't get why you never said anything to me. All that time, when you knew about me…"

"Grandpa thought I shouldn't. He says mers have been able to stay alive because we keep each other's secrets, which I guess kinda makes sense."

"I guess."

"We haven't really had much of a chance to talk about this whole mer stuff since Cori's pool party, and I know that's mostly my fault."

"No, wait a sec." I squeezed his hand for him to stop. "I need to apologize. I'm so sorry about jumping all over you yesterday. How's your mom. Is she doing okay?"

Luke nodded. "Yeah, thanks. We were all pretty freaked out for a while there, though. What about you? Any news about your mom?"

"Not really. It's kind of driving us nuts. My dad and I are planning a search and rescue mission tomorrow, though, to keep from going crazy."

"Anything I can do to help?"

"Got any contacts at the Mermish Council?" I asked hopefully.

"Hmm…" Luke considered this for a second. "If I knew what a Mermish Council was, maybe I could be more useful."

"I think it's in that mer handbook they forgot to give us." I laughed. "Anyway, I'm happy things worked out with your mom. And *really* happy I got to apologize before Cori strangled me with a dish towel."

"That Cori is *so* awesome, isn't she?" Luke said in an exaggerated tone as we continued walking.

"She told you to say that, didn't she?" I asked.

"Yep." Luke laughed.

Cori, Cori, Cori.

A warm ocean breeze swept up from Port Toulouse Bay, smelling of salt and summertime. The canal trail hooked up with the wooden boardwalk running along Toulouse Point Beach. Moms were out pushing jogging strollers along the boardwalk while a few guys tossed a football near the lifeguard tower. We reached the far end of the beach, where the sand gave way to a rocky shore that led to a point of giant granite boulders.

"So." We sat on a large log of silver-colored driftwood. "*Is* there actually a mer handbook? Because I'm mostly clueless when it comes to this mer stuff."

"Tell me about it." Luke leaned forward, resting his elbows on his knees.

"What do you mean?" I asked. "I thought you were the expert."

"Hardly." Luke looked out over the ocean, then glanced over his shoulder to me. "You remember the first time you crashed into me at Dooley's pharmacy?"

"Technically, you crashed into me, but yeah, I remember."

"I felt like there was something different about you that day, but I wasn't sure if it was you or because of what had just happened to me." Luke stood and crouched next to a puddle of ocean water left over from when the tide had gone out. He fished out a small crab. It waved its claws blindly in the air as Luke eyed it closely.

"You'd just gotten back from your sailing vacation with your family," I said.

"Yeah, but it was a bit more than just a vacation." Luke walked down to the edge of the water and placed the crab carefully in the water, then turned back to me.

"How so?" I asked.

"Well, my mom and dad had always told me I was adopted." He finger quoted *adopted*.

"So you always knew you were a mer?" I plucked a couple of starfish from the puddle and joined Luke at the edge of the water.

"Yeah, Grandpa was the one who found me washed up in a puddle like this when I was a baby." Luke shaded his eyes to look out into the ocean, then turned back to me. "At first, when I was little, I thought it was just a bed-time story, but when I was about nine, Mom, Dad, and

Grandpa explained it all to me. But it wasn't until this past spring that I knew what it all really meant. Grandpa knows another Webbed One in Florida…"

"A human who is part mer, like you and my mom, you mean?" I remembered the term *Webbed One* from Dad's *Mermaidia: Fact or Fiction* book. But Webbed Ones were far from fiction. In fact, Finalin and Medora had pulled me under the waters of Talisman Lake when they'd seen my webbed toes. "And me too, I guess."

"Yeah. So we sailed there to get help for my first time and everything."

"You mean, the first time you ever changed back to a mer since you were a baby was just this past spring?" I tossed the starfish into the water and wiped my hands on my shorts to dry them.

Luke nodded. "Yup."

Then, something occurred to me. Luke wasn't *exactly* like me. I was born human. And since my human DNA was so strong, I just had to crawl out of the water to change from mer *back* to human. Luke was different, though.

"So, if you're a Webbed One, but were born a mer, you must need a tidal pool to change back."

"Yeah. The tides in and out of a puddle like this were enough when I was a baby but the older you get the more complicated it becomes. There was a large pool on Bobby's property in Florida. We tried a few others, but they weren't as good and took much longer."

"Just like your grandpa told my dad. The pools aren't

really magical at all, are they?" Huh. Dad's Merlin 3000 sounded like it was on the right track. "So, how long does it take you to change exactly?"

"It gets easier each time. By the fourth time, I was down to about two days."

"Two days?" I asked.

"Yeah, why?" he asked. "How long does it take you?"

"No more than a couple minutes, but usually I puke or pass out."

Luke laughed and I'm sure I blushed, remembering the time he'd found me passed out next to Talisman Lake mid-transformation.

"This mer stuff is pretty nuts, huh? I'm still trying to figure out how I feel about it all." Luke turned to me and took my hand in his. He raised our hands in the air. "About this too. I hope that's okay?"

A warm feeling spread through my hand as I considered this for a second.

"So, what you're saying is that you're just as clueless as I am?" I asked.

"Pretty much." Luke dropped my hand and picked up a flat rock. He rubbed it between his thumb and index finger, then threw it over the water. It skipped a couple of times before sinking. He picked up another rock. "Things are just all really new for me too. What I could really use right now is a friend who gets where I'm coming from."

Friend. Was that a friend-friend or a kissy-friend I

wondered. But before I could ask, Luke stopped tossing his rock mid-throw.

"Do you hear that?" He looked over his shoulder at me.

"What?" I listened, but all I could hear was the sound of waves washing up along the shore. But then the wind changed and I heard it too—a high-pitched whine like the sound of a motorboat. "What is that?"

Luke tossed his rock aside and strode down the beach. I followed. "Wait, Luke. What's making that noise?"

Luke broke into a run and headed for the breakwater, calling over his shoulder, "It's Reese!"

"Owrch!" I stubbed my toe on a rock, trying to catch up. Who the heck was Reese?

Chapter Five

B Y THE TIME I reached Luke, he'd already scrambled up onto the rocky breakwater jutting out into the ocean and was hopping from one enormous boulder to another.

"Wait! Luke!" I yelled, afraid of what he might do. Thankfully, we were at least a quarter of a mile from the main part of the public beach, but still. With the pounding surf and jagged rocks, this was not the best place to plunge into the depths of the Atlantic Ocean, even if you were a pesco-sapien. "Be careful!"

"Come on!" Luke waved an arm over his head before jumping down and disappearing behind a rock.

"Luke!" I called out, worried he'd hopped into the ocean and was sprouting a tail by then. I caught my flip-flop in a crack trying to climb a boulder to get to him, scraping my big toe in the process (again!). "Ow, ow, ow! I do *not* have the right shoes for this."

Thankfully, I found Luke on a low-lying rock near the end of the point. He had a hand to his ear, straining to hear over the sound of waves crashing all around us.

"What the heck are you trying to do? Get us both killed?" I stepped down beside him and hung onto a nearby boulder to avoid getting swept out to sea by a random wave.

"Where *is* he?" Luke shaded his eyes and scanned the water.

"This is a bad idea." I turned to go.

"No, I swear I heard him. Just wait a second." Luke caught my arm to stop me.

"Heard who, exactly?"

Reese! Luke called out into the vastness of the ocean. His mer voice came out as a high-pitched ring, like the sound of buzzing electrical wires or summer cicadas.

"I'm guessing this Reese guy is a mer, but how the heck do you even know him?" I asked. "Other than when you were a baby, you just said you've only transitioned to a mer once this past spring. In Florida!"

Luke turned and laughed when he saw I was clinging onto the boulder for dear life. "I met Reese way before that."

"But how?"

"I didn't actually meet him. I heard him." Luke pounced onto the next rock, searching the waters as he went. "My mom and dad used to take us down here for picnics all the time. Trey and I would jump from rock to rock like this for hours. One day, my ears rang like crazy and Mom and Dad thought it was because I was listening to my music too loud. But that wasn't it. I could hear him. I could hear Reese."

"How do you even know his name?" I pulled a wind-blown strand of hair from my mouth.

"I don't. That's just the sound he made whenever he came by. Trey never saw him, but once I figured out how to make the sound back to him, Reese would swim by my rock every once in a while—to check me out, I guess."

I scanned the waters for any signs of life, but all I could make out was a motorboat heading toward the canal and a harbor seal swimming a few dozen feet away.

"Ohmigod! Luke, there's an actual *seal* right over there." I pointed. "This would *not* be a good time to fall in." I shrank back as far from the edge of the rock as possible, just in case seals ate people.

I couldn't make out how big and potentially scary the seal was from that far away, but thankfully, it turned its head toward us and then flicked away.

"No, no! That's him," Luke said. *Reese! It's me! It's Luke!*

A dark figure zigzagged toward us just below the surface of the water. The surf made it hard to spot as it swam, but soon the figure was beside our boulder and, sure enough, it wasn't a seal. It was the chubbiest mer-dude I'd ever seen. Compared to the pasty-looking Freshies from Talisman Lake, this guy looked healthy and extremely well-fed.

Lukshh? Reese hung on the edge of our rock to keep from being swept away by the tide. He looked about our age and his long hair swirled around his full face, which broke into a smile once he got a good look at Luke.

Lukrshh! Reese rang up to Luke, then pointed to me.

Jade, Luke answered, as he pulled my hand into his. We

both crouched down on the rock to get a better look at Reese. *This is Jade.*

Reese nodded. *Ja-shhde.* He glanced at Luke then pointed to himself and rang *Reesshh,* as if to say Luke's nickname suited him just fine.

Luke rang a couple sounds I didn't recognize.

"What are you saying to him? Wait. How do you even know how to speak Mermish?" I asked, wondering if there was some online Mermish-to-English translator I'd never heard of.

"I don't really," Luke said, turning to me. "I just picked up the basics when I was with Bobby in Florida."

"Bobby? The mer your grandpa hooked you up with?" I let out a huge snort. Reese and Luke glanced at me with puzzled looks.

Bobby bobbing in the water? I rang out to both of them. *What? It's funny!*

Fneeee, Reese rang back and smiled, then he swam around our rock, diving and darting around. Something caught his eye on the ocean floor. He picked it up and examined it, then stashed it in a satchel-like woven bag strung across his chest.

I whispered to Luke, "I'll say one thing: the guy really has an ear for languages. You too, by the way."

"You'll pick up Mermish too, don't worry. It's pretty close to Spanish if you listen closely," Luke said.

"Spanish?" I moaned. I hated Spanish. "Sounds more like nails on a chalkboard to me."

"Bobby thinks the high pitch blocks fishermen's sonar signals, so it's not all bad," Luke said. "It's the only way we've been able to hide from them for the past century."

So all the hi-tech gadgets on the Martins' boat wouldn't help us one bit. What was the point of going out with Dad the next day if we weren't going to find anything anyway?

"Hey, do you think Reese knows anything about my mom?"

"I'll ask." Luke turned to Reese and they exchanged a few rings.

Yes, mother. Then, Luke pointed to me. *Daughter.* He made a few signs with his hands and rang a few more sounds. Reese nodded as though he understood and rang back.

"He says his uncle might know something." Luke kicked off his shoes. "Come on, we should go check it out."

Just then, a humongous wave crashed onto our rock, soaking us to the skin. I lunged for the boulder beside us and worked to get my heart back in my chest cavity.

"*Might* know something? Nuh-uh, nuh-uh, nuh-uh… let's think this thing through a little bit. I mean, what if his uncle is an ax murderer or a homicidal maniac or a merman cannibal or something?" I knew I was babbling, but the hugeness of the ocean was seriously creeping me out. Dad was right. Next stop: England.

Luke raised an eyebrow and laughed. "Cannibal? Seriously?"

"Look. Reese seems like a nice guy and everything, but there's no way we should be going anywhere with a mer we just met."

Reese looked up and glanced from Luke to me as if trying to figure out what we were talking about.

"Okay, okay," Luke said. "If it makes you feel better, you stay here and I'll go."

"Um…did you forget you need a tidal pool to change back?" I asked. "That wouldn't really help our cause."

"Oh, right. But we might not get this chance again."

"Fine, okay." Reluctantly, I released my death grip on the rock and kicked off my flip-flops. Dad was going to kill me, but Luke was right. I couldn't pass up this chance. "If anyone is going to get eaten by a merman cannibal, trying to find my mom, it might as well be me."

"Are you sure?" Luke asked.

"Nope." If I dove in and breathed in the water—especially *salt*water—it was tail city and there was no turning back. But I hated swimming. I hated being wet. Could I take the plunge and become a mermaid again?

But if Reese knew someone who might know what was happening with Mom, I'd have to suck it up. I crouched down on the rock and tried to see where Reese had gone through the ocean surf.

Hey, Reese. Can you get me to your uncle before dinnertime? I joked, flashing the face of my Day-Glo Timex his way to show the time.

Reese swam up to me. He reached out of the water and took my wrist in his hands to inspect my digital watch. He looked at me with an eager smile as if asking permission to touch the buttons.

Knock yourself out, I rang in English. I took off the watch and attached it to Reese's chubby outstretched arm. Maybe if I gave him a peace offering he wouldn't drag me to their town center and hang me over a pot of fish chowder. *So we can go?*

Go-rrsh. He smiled, staring at the watch.

No, that's a watch, I explained patiently. I looked up at Luke. "Give him yours too. That way at least he'll feel bad when he leads me to my death."

"No way, this is a really expensive diving watch." Luke put his hand over his watch as if to protect it.

"Way to take one for the team!" I whacked his leg.

"Sorry!" Luke laughed and rubbed his leg. "My grandpa gave it to me. He'll kill me if I lose it."

"Fine, but if I get bumped off, I'm blaming you." I turned to Reese. *Now can we go?*

Go-rshh! Reese swam away then looked over his shoulder for me to follow.

You do realize you just said that partly in Mermish, don't you? Luke held out his hand and pulled me to my feet.

I looked at him, not quite understanding what he was saying, mostly because he was speaking Mermish too. That's when I realized I was kind of getting it!

"Cool. I'll get Reese to teach me all the swear words," I joked, but my stomach cramped as I wondered what I was getting myself into. Sure, Reese seemed nice enough, but I'd watched enough horror movies to know that the ax-wielding, head-bludgeoning villain always seemed nice enough at the *beginning* of the movie. "I'll teach you if I make it back."

"Hey." Luke grasped my arm and pulled me into a hug. "I'll be right here waiting, okay?" he murmured into my hair.

"Okay," I replied, my voice barely a whisper. My heart pounded hard enough that I was sure Luke could hear it, and a warm feeling of hopefulness spread through my body. I gathered up my courage and stepped to the edge of the boulder, taking one last look around to make sure no one was watching before making the big plunge.

"Get me a new pair of shorts for when I get backrrppp…!" I called out as I dove, but the sound came out in a glob of bubbles, forcing a shot of saltwater down my throat. The water stung my eyes and burned my nostrils. Something disgusting and slimy, which I could only imagine was a jelly-fish, swept by me, sending a sting of pain along my forearm.

Just breathe. Breathe, I told myself, but all I could do was gag as I kicked and pulled at the water to dive deeper. It had been almost a month since the last time I'd turned into a mermaid, in Talisman Lake, and the expression "like a fish to water" definitely did *not* apply to me.

Where the heck are…? I found my mer-voice and called out for Reese into the dark, murky water. I caught a glimpse of a tail about twenty feet away, deeper into the bay. But before my eyes could completely focus on what I'd just seen, my sudden legs-to-tail transformation blew my shorts to smithereens and sent me hurtling through the water.

Ooorff! I fell back against the rocky bottom of the ocean, whacking my head in the process. So, yeah, with a jellyfish sting along my arm and a concussion to the head, plus the fact that the ocean looked like a big black hole, I was seriously wondering if I'd made a giant mistake. I let the water pass through my mouth and nose, and inhaled deeply to catch my breath. Surprisingly, it felt like a gulp of fresh spring air, a huge difference from the mucky water of Talisman Lake.

Just then, something else brushed against my other arm. *Ahhh!* I yelled.

Hello. Reese appeared beside me carrying his satchel, which I could now tell was made with the plastic rings that hold six-packs of soda, sewn together with some sort of twine. He stared in amazement and swam around me in dizzying loops and dives, like an otter I saw at the zoo when I was a kid. *You are a Webbed One!*

Yes, yes. The fairy tales you heard as a kid are true, I said in my broken Mermish, but Reese got the gist once Luke translated from his perch on the rock overhead.

Okay! We go-rshh. Ready? Reese asked, swimming ahead.

Was I ready? If I looked back to the beach, I was fine, despite the swaying jellyfish, mossy rocks, and swirling sand; but out into the ocean was a sea of random fish, plunging cormorants, then nothingness.

But this could be my one and only chance to find Mom.

As ready as I'll ever be. I waved to Luke one last time and swam to catch up as Reese raced ahead.

For a chubby mer, the guy was surprisingly fast.

Chapter Six

WE DIDN'T HAVE TO go very far to find Reese's uncle—just a short swim across the length of the Toulouse Point Beach to the mouth of the boat canal leading up to Talisman Lake, as a matter of fact. That's when it became pretty obvious I was about to run into some old pals if I wasn't careful.

I hung back, darting from one swaying clump of sea-weed to another, trying to keep the canal sentries in my sights without being seen. I couldn't tell for sure, but they looked like the same sentries I had had to escape from with my mom and Serena a few weeks before.

Reese swam back to see why I wasn't following quite so closely anymore.

Uncle. Uncle Alzear. Reese motioned to one of the two mermen patrolling the mouth of the canal.

A sentry? Your uncle is a sentry?

Yes, uncle. Reese searched my face. *Find mother?*

Yes. Yes, I want to find my mother, but it would probably be better if they didn't see me. I looked down at the T-shirt

I was still wearing compared to everyone else's bare chest. Surely, that would be a dead giveaway that I wasn't from around there. Reese seemed to understand. *Ask your uncle— could you ask him if he knows anything about a tidal pool?*

Reese squinted. *Tidal pool?*

Yes, I replied, making a sweeping motion with my arms to try to explain. *Water pool. Tides. In and out.*

Reese nodded and grasped the strap of his satchel, then swam up to the mouth of the canal. The sentries swam up to meet him, holding their spears across their chests. Uncle Alzear put a hand on Reese's shoulder while the other one yelled at him.

Restricted. You cannot be here!

I flinched at the sound of his piercing ring but tried to stay hidden while peering through a clump of swaying seaweed. Uncle Alzear put his hand up to stop the other sentry, then spoke quietly in Reese's ear. Reese shook his head as if to say he wouldn't go, then turned to the other sentry. He offered him several things from his satchel but none seemed to be of any interest. Finally, Reese unclasped my watch from his wrist and held it out to him.

Geesh, that was a forty-dollar Timex, I muttered.

The sentry smiled with all four of his teeth, attached the watch to his spear, then swam back up the canal, but not before glancing back to flash Uncle Alzear a warning look.

Reese and his uncle spoke, but their backs were turned, so it was hard to tell what they were saying. Uncle Alzear shook his head a lot but Reese persisted. Finally, Reese motioned in my direction. I ducked behind a large clump of swaying kelp to avoid being seen. By the time I had the nerve to risk a peek a few minutes later, Reese was swimming to my side.

Are you crazy? He could have seen me, I whispered in a low ring once he slipped behind the kelp with me, hidden from view.

Reese fiddled with the closure of his satchel. *Did not see you.*

So, what did he say? Does he know about the tidal pool? I asked. But from the smile on Reese's face, I could tell the answer was yes. I put a hand to my mouth. Could it be? Was I that much closer to finding Mom? *Where? Where is it?*

Reese glanced around to get his bearings, then turned to the western coastline, past the canal and away from Toulouse Point.

Can you take me there? How far is it? I asked, trying to keep my tone low despite my growing excitement.

Reese let out a series of rings, none of which I could understand.

Whoa. Slow down. What are you saying?

Reese fumbled around in his satchel and pulled out a Happy Meal toy still in its packaging, pointing to the large M emblazoned on the plastic packaging.

I turned the toy over and examined it. Seawater had seeped into the package but the blue plastic figurine inside was still intact. I recognized it from a movie I'd seen advertised the spring before.

There was only one McDonald's anywhere near Port Toulouse. I looked at Reese and raised an eyebrow. *The McDonald's by the mall?*

Reese pointed at the toy again, as if he figured I hadn't understood.

No, no—I get it. Okay, the mall it is. Let's go!

Go-rshh. Reese stuffed the toy back in his satchel and smiled, then took my hand to head westward.

I glanced over my shoulder and quickly turned away when I saw Uncle Alzear watching us swim off, his spear held loosely by his side.

We swam for miles—nautical miles, which I was sure were ten times farther than actual miles.

The thought of Mom kept me going despite how big and scary the ocean seemed compared to Talisman Lake. The whole saltwater experience had its pluses, though. I could see better, hear better, and actually understood what Reese was saying more and more as he gave me a guided ocean tour. We stuck to the coast, where the kelp was thicker to hide me from view, and swam along the ocean floor, around outcroppings of rock covered with mosses and crawling shellfish. I saw a humongous green lobster the size of a preschooler snatch a passing mackerel in its massive claw.

Note to self: Stay away from scary, snapping lobsters.

We followed a school of mackerel for a while, which was kind of cool, until I realized the floaty bits swirling behind them were probably chunks of uneaten flesh or digested food, and I got totally grossed out and gagged at the thought of breathing in that stuff.

My tail ached and my arms were about to fall off by the time Reese slowed down long enough for me to catch up. I spotted the big golden McDonald's arches off in the distance.

Holy Chicken McNuggets. We actually made it. We—

But before I could finish my sentence, something whizzed by my head.

Reese pushed me out of the way. *Stay down!*

What the heck was that? We ducked behind an outcropping of rock covered with swaying seaweed. *Who's after us?*

Not sure. Reese parted the seaweed with one hand so we could get a better look. The projectiles kept whizzing by us but missed us by a mile, judging by the streams of bubbles a dozen feet away.

Either they're not shooting at us or they have really bad aim, I rang in a low tone.

Seconds later, a *PING* sounded through the water. The shooting stopped.

You're late! A deep mer-voice rang from a couple dozen feet away. I peeked around the rock. A large grizzly looking merman brandishing a spear swam to meet a small elderly mermaid.

Yeah, well, tell that to your goon friends, the mermaid replied. *They wrecked my stall back at the market looking for contraband. It will take me days to get it back in order.*

It's Renata, Reese whispered. *With food.*

Renata held out a package wrapped in seaweed to Grizzly while another sentry hung back by a large underwater metal culvert by the shore, which was probably where the projectile had hit to cause the sound. Could they be guarding the entry to the tidal pool, keeping the Webbed Ones in and the rubberneckers out? My breath quickened as I thought of the possibility. What if we were finally about to discover Mom, but they caught us before we could get to her?

The merman by the culvert called out to Renata with a friendly wave. *Any squid today, Renata?*

Got some right here for you, Omarlin! She searched in her sleigh-like cart and tried to swim toward the culvert to bring it to him, but Grizzly blocked her with his spear.

You know the rules. He took the squid from her and piled it on top of the package she'd already given him. *I'll take it from here.* He turned to go.

What? No tip? Renata rang after him. But Grizzly ignored her, swam back to the culvert, and disappeared inside. Omarlin smiled weakly and waved, then disappeared into the darkness of the culvert too.

Renata rang out a bunch of sentences, which I was pretty sure were mer-curse words, and stooped over to arrange the rest of the packages in her cart.

My stomach cramped with anticipation and worry.

This is it, I whispered to Reese. *This must be the entrance to the tidal pool. Only problem is how do we get in?*

But just then, another rumble gurgled from my stomach. All the excitement had set Bridget's lunchtime cheesy nachos into motion. Roiling, gurgling, cramping. This couldn't be happening. Not now!

No matter how hard I tried to control it, a mixture of nerves, fear, jalapenos, and bad timing all came together in a stomach-rumbling, gas-producing…*mwuuurppppp*.

A huge burp bubble escaped from my mouth and traveled past my face, up and over the rock and seaweed where we were hiding.

Excuse me, I whispered.

Reese flashed me an odd, approving smile. I couldn't help it. An uncontrollable urge to giggle took over me just like it always did whenever Cori and I were at a really serious school assembly. It started as a jittery feeling in my chest and escaped as a massive underwater snort. If Renata hadn't seen my burp bubble, I was sure this would blow our cover. I poked my head around the rock to check.

Who's there? Renata scanned the waters around her and slipped out a slingshot-looking weapon from between the packages in her cart.

What do we do now? I whispered.

Reese said nothing but rifled through his satchel. I peeked in and counted four flip-flops, a waterlogged cell phone, and about six gold chains.

Where did you get all this stuff? I picked out an ID wallet and wondered what poor sap had lost it. Bridget Lavoie according to the expired driver's license. Bridget's

Diner–Bridget? I stifled another laugh. I bet my boss would never guess her ID had been stolen by an underwater kleptomaniac.

Reese took the wallet back from me and stashed it in his satchel. He hesitated for a moment, looking like he wondered whether he could trust me. *Beach. From tides,* he said carefully.

I said, who's there? Renata said once again, this time more forcefully.

You stay here, Reese whispered to me and pulled out one of the flip-flops. *She likes these.*

Renata turned as Reese slipped out from our hiding spot. *Stay hidden!* she hissed, glancing over her shoulder to the culvert to make sure no one was looking.

Reese swam slickly to another clump of kelp nearby while Renata busied herself, packing items into her cart, keeping her back to the culvert.

You can't be here, she said in a low ring.

What is this place? Reese asked from his new hiding place. *Is this the tidal pool?*

Renata stared at the clump of kelp and quickly turned back to her work. *You do not know what you are asking.*

I stayed behind my rock, quite sure I didn't want anyone popping out of the culvert and skewering us with their spears, but I had to know.

How do we get through there? I called out to her.

Renata scanned the waters around her. *Who have you brought with you?*

Reese slipped out from his hiding place and looked my way, shaking his head slightly to signal me to stay hidden.

A friend. He took the flip-flop and tied it onto Renata's cart. That's when I noticed all the other ocean-weathered flip-flops adorning the cart's side like a string of colorful banners. *A friend looking for her mother.*

Renata touched Reese's arm for a moment and sighed. She looked back at the culvert. *Tell your friend no one gets through there. Last one who tried now has to pick his nose with his thumbs. I can't even come close, that's why I have to shoot barnacles from this far away to signal I'm here. Don't stay here,* Renata continued. *The shift changes soon, then you'll have four sentries to fend off instead of two.* She stored the slingshot in her cart, then turned to pick up the cart's handles so she could drag it behind her.

Before Renata could swim away, her prediction came true and two other sentries blasted onto the scene, screeching like a couple of riot police.

What is your business here?

Very serious breach!

Under arrest!

One grabbed Reese around the neck in a headlock while the other held Renata's hands behind her back. I almost hurtled out of my hiding spot to help them, but Reese caught my eye and mouthed no, urging me to stay put. I slipped back down, afraid of what the sentries might do to Reese and Renata and wishing I could do something to help.

But by then, Grizzly and Omarlin had slipped out of the culvert to see what the commotion was all about.

Take your posts at the entry, Grizzly ordered to the new sentries as he swam to meet them. The newcomers handed Renata and Reese off to Omarlin and Grizzly before disappearing through the mouth of the culvert. Reese winced as Grizzly tied long strands of twine-like seaweed around his wrists. *As for you two, we'll let the Mermish Council decide what to do with you.*

My heart broke in a million pieces as they dragged Renata and Reese away.

Chapter Seven

IT TOOK ME TWICE as long to swim back to Toulouse Point without Reese as my guide. It didn't help that I was completely paranoid and had to dart from one hiding place to another to keep from getting spotted. By the time I'd snuck past the mouth of the canal, I was so exhausted I could barely move my tail.

I wanted to cry when I thought of everything that had just happened. What would happen to Renata? Or Reese? They'd both sacrificed so much to help me, only to find the tidal pool locked up tighter than Alcatraz. Was it even the tidal pool at all? What if the trip was actually a dead end and the sentries were hiding something else past that culvert? Now Reese and Renata were both in big-time trouble and it was all my fault.

I sighed in relief when I recognized the spot where I'd kicked off my flip-flops at Toulouse Point. Only problem was Luke was nowhere in sight.

Okay, universe! I rang out into the ocean, beyond caring who could hear me at that point. *I could really use a break right now, you know!*

Tell me about it.

I spun around in the water, trying to spot the source of the voice. It wasn't until I'd swum around the point to the other side when I finally saw Luke standing on the rocky shore. And Cori was with him.

Oh no. What is she doing here? I rang out.

Cori held a cell phone to her ear and looked like she was trying to make a call. Luke kept tugging at her arm, trying to reason with her, but Cori held firm.

I lifted my head out of the water just enough so I could hear, doubting Cori could see me through the choppy waves.

"You found her wallet and her cell. What other proof do you need?" She shrugged Luke's hand away. "Something's wrong here, Luke. We have to call someone!"

"I'm sure she's fine." Luke grappled with her in a comical display of arm flapping and hand flailing, trying to get the phone away from her. "But here, let me call."

"I think I know how to use a cell phone, Luke." Cori held the phone up in the air and squinted at the screen like she was trying to get reception, but thankfully it looked like the sand dunes and boulders were blocking her phone signal. "When are they ever going to put another cell tower in this town?"

We'd better do something before she gets the whole Port Toulouse Emergency Response Team out here, Luke rang.

I should get out—should I get out? I hesitated, remembering what Dad had told me about telling other people about my mermaid secret. Cori would freak if she found out about me. I'd told her a little about what I was going through back at her pool party. I even admitted that it had something to do with Mom, but there was no way she would ever guess the real reason behind all my freakiness. Did I really want to open that can of worms? *Maybe she'll leave soon.*

Um, she doesn't look like she's going anywhere. Luke scrambled after Cori as she climbed a large rock jutting partway into the ocean, looking for better reception. I laughed as she stretched up on her tippy-toes, turning this way and that way while Luke urged her to get down. She waved him away but in the process, managed to slip off the rock.

"Hel-uphtt!" Cori yelled. But her cry was muffled as she hit the water with an impressive splash.

Cori! I rang out, but of course she couldn't hear me. A powerful force took over, making me forget everything my dad ever told me about keeping my identity a secret. I had to get to her!

Within seconds, I had Cori around the waist and I was dragging her to shore. She lay limp in my arms as I swam with all my might to get her to safety.

You got her! Luke rang.

I think she banged her head. My face broke the surface of the water just as Luke splashed into the ocean to meet us.

I coughed up a lungful of water and gasped as the early evening air burned my lungs. Luke dragged Cori to shore and checked her pulse and breathing, which was good, because I was as useless as a beached tuna from where I was sitting, waist deep in the ocean.

"Is she okay?!" I called out between sputters and coughs as Luke turned Cori over to her side just as she was coming to.

"Ja—?" Cori's eyelids fluttered as she put her cell phone to her ear, which she (amazingly) still had clutched in her hand. Leave it to Cori to stay connected through a near-death experience. Luke pried the phone away from her and waved his hand for me to hide before Cori started really coming around.

But I couldn't move. My mermaid-to-girl transformation had begun and the pain grabbed me like vice. My lungs burned like someone was forcing steam down my throat and the scales on my tail stung and grew hot as they turned back into skin.

"Jade?" Cori rubbed her head as she sat up on the beach and squinted through half-closed eyes.

Luke looked at me hopelessly and did his best to get Cori to her feet, but she shrugged him away and walked slowly toward me, stumbling a bit as she shook off the wooziness.

"There you are! What are you doing sitting in the water?" Cori looked out over the ocean, then back at me, trying to figure out what she was seeing. "Were you swimming? Why were you swimming all by yourself?"

Just then, Trey came running down the shore, looking like he'd just mowed a lawn, judging by his grass-stained work boots. He waved a pair of sweat pants over his head.

"I couldn't find any girl shorts but these might fit." He stopped short when he saw Cori. "Uh-oh."

"Girl shorts?" Cori was wide-awake now. She glanced at the rock she'd been standing on, trying to process what had just happened. "Wait a second…I fell in the water…" She turned to me. "You rescued me…you had a…"

There was no turning back now. I lifted my searing hot tail out of the water.

"A tail, you mean?"

This time Cori *did* pass out. Good thing Trey was right behind her to help break her fall.

By the time Cori came around, my legs were back and I'd managed to get the sweatpants on after threatening Trey and Luke with bodily harm if they so much as glanced my way.

"Okay. I'm decent." I came out of my hiding spot behind one of the granite boulders and tried to get my balance on my newly regenerated feet.

I slipped on my flip-flops and quickly explained what was going on with Reese and Mom to Trey and Luke as Cori groaned on the ground, not quite conscious yet.

"I'm so sorry about Reese, Luke."

Luke stared out over the ocean. "No, I'm the one who's sorry. I should never have let you go all by yourself."

Yes, it was childish and maybe I was verging on a mental breakdown after what had just happened, but something about what Luke said ticked me off.

"*Let me?*" I squeezed the front of my shirt to try to get rid of some of the dampness, then got my wallet and phone from him. "Last time I checked, I didn't need your permission."

Weren't we just friends, after all?

"Sorry." Luke closed his eyes and shook his head. "That's not what I meant."

"Easy, easy!" Trey held up his hands like a referee at a hockey game. "Let's focus for a second, shall we? At least now you know where the tidal pool is."

"Where it *might* be. But how are we supposed to find out if we can't get through the culvert?" I checked my phone and saw the six missed texts from Cori. It was also past five o'clock. Dad would be calling any second to see if I needed a ride home after my supposed shift at the ice cream parlor.

Sure enough, Cori was just showing signs of life when my phone rang.

"Dad." What was I going to tell him? He was going to ground me well into my thirties if he found out I'd just spent the afternoon underwater without his permission, especially after the conversation we'd just had the day before. Should I tell him about the culvert and get his hopes up? But who knew if the culvert actually led to the tidal pool?

"Jade! Where are you? I dropped by Bridget's to pick you up but she said you got off hours ago." I could hear the panic in his voice. I couldn't make him worry more.

"I'm fine, Dad. Just hanging out with Cori and the gang."

Trey and Luke waved their hands in the air at me. Trey pretended to eat a hamburger. Luke traced a giant M in the air with his fingers. A smile grew on my lips, realizing what they were planning. "Uh, Dad? We were thinking of grabbing a burger at McDonald's. Is that okay?"

By then, Cori was at my side, gaping at me as I spoke to Dad. "What happened to me? Why was I passed out on the beach?" she whispered.

I waved my hand in front of my face and made a *shh* motion as I tried to listen to Dad's response.

"I can give you kids a ride over. Where are you? I'll come pick you up."

"Oh, no. That's okay. We'll take the bus."

"Okay, but don't stay out too late. Remember, we've got a big day tomorrow," Dad said.

"I won't," I replied, feeling a little bit guilty that he was still planning the next day's Mer-to-Mom rescue mission.

"And be careful!" he added.

"I will! Love you." I hung up and looked at the phone for a minute, wondering whether I was making the right choice by waiting to clue him in to what was going on, before turning to Luke and Trey. "Okay, okay. No use getting my dad's hopes up if the culvert just leads to a secret mer-mobster hideout instead of a magical tidal pool."

Cori was still looking at me as if I were telling a really suspenseful horror story, like we used to do at summer camp. But this had better have a happier ending than my famous campfire slasher stories where everyone ended up with an ax embedded in their skull.

"Magical wha...? What the heck are you saying?" Cori snapped to attention. "'Mer' as in *mermaid*? Is that why you were sitting in the water? And did I imagine it or did I actually see you with a *tail*?"

I flipped my phone shut and grabbed Cori by the arm. "Come on! I'll explain on the way."

Chapter Eight

The bus to the mall made about nine hundred stops so Cori had plenty of time to give me the third degree.

"So, let me get this straight," she whispered. We sat in the last two seats of the bus, away from the elderly couple at the front and the group of older teenagers zoned out on their iPods by the middle doors. "You're telling me you're part mermaid and that Luke here is also a mer-boy and you just spent the afternoon underwater with a *tail*? Did I miss anything?"

"Nope, I think you pretty much have everything covered," I whispered back. Then I considered everything and smiled broadly. "Oh, and I inherited my mermaid genes from my mom—who is very much alive last time I checked, by the way."

"Your *mother* is a mermaid? You mean she never drowned?" Cori's eyes were so wide I was afraid her eyeballs would pop out. "How long have you known all this?"

"I found out the week we went bathing suit shopping at Hyde's." I spotted the sign for Port Toulouse Mall as the bus turned off the highway.

"But that was back in June!" Cori cried.

A girl at the middle doors pulled an ear bud from her ear. "Do you mind?"

Cori mumbled an apology and turned to the window, resting her forehead on the glass.

"I'm really sorry, Cori," I said quietly once the girl went back to her music. "I begged my dad to tell you, but he swore me to secrecy. He was afraid scientists would treat me like a lab rat freak if they found out."

"Like some kind of science experiment, you mean?" Cori asked, turning from the window.

"Or worse," I replied, remembering the story in the book *Mermaidia: Fact or Fiction* about the Webbed One who was locked up in a mental hospital and given shock therapy.

Cori considered this for a second.

"I guess when you put it that way…" she said reluctantly.

"So do you forgive me for keeping it a secret?" I asked.

"I'll think about it. But only because your dad made you." Then she slapped Trey's shoulder. "But you! You knew all this and didn't tell me?"

"Not my secret to tell, dude," Trey said, turning in his seat. "That's what our grandpa says, anyway."

"True. All true," Luke agreed, giving his brother a fist bump.

"Your grandpa? Does everyone in Port Toulouse know about this except me?" Cori asked.

"Not exactly, so you can't tell anyone, okay?" I whispered.

"Who would I tell?" Cori raised her hands in the air and shook her head. "Who would believe me?"

"You've got to promise, Cori." Luke turned in his seat to look at her. "Please?"

Cori took a deep breath. "If this means Jade might actually find her mother again, I absolutely promise," she replied.

"Cool." I nudged her shoulder and rang to Luke.

Thanks, and I'm sorry for earlier.

Don't mention it, he rang back. *It's been a bit of a crazy day.*

Ringing back and forth with Luke in our mer voices reminded me of the first time I'd found out he was mer at Cori's pool party. To us, it sounded like our normal voices but in another frequency. To others, it was an irritating buzz. Cori pulled her phone out of her bag and put it to her ear.

"What is that annoying sound?" Cori stared at her phone when she realized it hadn't rung.

We'd finally arrived at the mall.

"Maybe it's from the construction," I said. Luke smiled.

The bus drove past the theater, along the length of the mall toward the Hyde's Department Store entrance at the far side of the parking lot, but there was a bunch of heavy equipment and chain-link fencing, making it hard to get around. Finally, the bus stopped and we all piled out.

"Uh-oh." I nudged Cori as we stepped onto the sidewalk.

"What? Oh." Cori tensed as Lainey Chamberlain exited the mall entrance and walked toward us, carrying about fourteen shopping bags. Lainey was in our grade at school.

She'd had her eye on Luke back in the spring and was not exactly keen on the fact that he'd chosen me over her. Cori had stood up to her in my defense during Luke's end-of-school boat cruise when she found out Lainey had given me the nickname Scissor Lips back in the fifth grade. They hadn't spoken since.

"Jade." Lainey stopped in front of me, then scanned the rest of our group. "Trey, Luke...and Cori Blake." She said Cori's name as if chewing on a piece of steak.

Trey and Luke waved and disappeared across the parking lot to McDonald's, leaving us to speak to Lainey. I couldn't decide if they were yellow-bellied cowards or just really sensible.

"Be nice," I muttered to Cori.

"Hi, Lainey," Cori said brightly. "How's your summer so far?"

"Spec-tac-u-lar," Lainey said, pronouncing each syllable. She dropped her bags at the curb and pulled out her cell phone from a really fancy looking handbag. "Just got back from New York. The shopping was ah-mazing. Mother wanted to go check out the upcoming winter trends for her new boutique."

"Looks like you've been busy shopping here too." I nodded to her bags, trying to change the subject since Cori had hoped to actually *work* at Mrs. Chamberlain's boutique before her big blowout with Lainey.

"Oh, this mall is *so* bad. It will be much better once my daddy finishes the new wing construction."

That's when I saw the sign.

CHAMBERLAIN CONSTRUCTION PRESENTS:
PORT TOULOUSE MALL EXPANSION
USING ONLY ENVIRONMENTALLY FRIENDLY
BUILDING PRODUCTS
GOING GREEN TO SERVE YOU BETTER!

"Well, gotta go! Oh, Jade." Lainey glanced down at my oversized sweatpants and made a face. "Sport Mart is having a back-to-school sale. Might want to check it out." A long black sedan pulled up in front of the mall and Lainey picked up her bags before disappearing inside.

"That girl is pure evil." Cori stared at the car as it pulled away.

"Yeah, sorry you had to lose your internship at her mom's boutique because of me."

Cori squinted. "How do you know about that?" Then, she looked at me wide-eyed. "Are mermaids telepathic? Can you tell what I'm thinking right now?"

"No." I laughed. "I was underneath the Descousse Marina pier with my mom, growing legs, when you and Lainey had your big fight. Heard the whole thing."

Cori shook her head. "This cannot be real."

"It's all pavement and buildings around here," Luke said when they returned. "Are you sure this is right?"

I glanced at the McDonald's across the parking lot, closer to the road.

"It has to be. I could see the golden arches from the water." I looked around for some open space where a tidal pool might be.

Cori stood on the sidewalk as the bus pulled away, still muttering about how she couldn't believe what was happening. Finally she looked around, trying to get her bearings.

"So what are we doing at the mall exactly?" Cori asked.

"Looking for a magical tidal pool," Luke whispered in her ear, trying to hold back a smile.

I laughed. It was kind of fun to mess with her head.

"I'm going to pretend I didn't hear that." Cori put her fingers in her ears and hummed.

"Maybe it's closer to the mall," Trey suggested.

We walked up to the chain-link fence by the construction site and tried to look between the signs advertising the mall expansion. Could the tidal pool be in there? Was Mom just inside that fence? "I can't see past these signs."

Just then, a car backfired in the parking lot, making Cori jump in surprise.

"I seriously don't know how much more of this I can take." She put a hand to her chest.

Seconds later, a great blue heron rose from within the construction site a few hundred feet away.

"Herons usually mean there's water!" Luke said.

"Let's get past these signs to get a better look," I suggested, hoping Luke was right.

The fence stretched from the mall by Hyde's and continued for several hundred yards toward the ocean. We followed it through a marshy area and down to a secondary gravel road that ran along the shore.

"It looks like the fence goes along this road then turns back up to the mall in a big rectangle," Trey said.

I looked back up the hill toward the mall and could still make out the McDonald's golden arches off in the distance, just like earlier, underwater. "Does anyone see a culvert around here?"

"There's a bit of a hump in the road up ahead," Luke said.

Luke and I followed the raised ground across to where the ocean met the large rocks at the shoulder of the road. We climbed the rocks and peered into the deep water.

"Do you see anything?" Trey called from the road where he waited with Cori.

"Yes!" I yelled. "But it's under a couple feet of water."

It was the same gray metal tunnel I'd seen with Reese. We'd found it! Now, how were we supposed to get through it?

"How big were those mer-dude's spears?" Luke asked as we turned back to join Cori and Trey on the dirt road.

"Big!" I said, shivering at the thought. "So, unless we want to get skewered, we're going to have to find another way in."

"Mer-dudes with spears?!" Cori cried, scanning the open ocean. "Next you'll be telling me to watch out for sea witches."

"I haven't seen any sea witches yet, but there's a pretty scary mermaid named Medora in Talisman Lake." I searched for the hump in the road again and followed it as it ran straight through to the construction site. I peered through the fence. The evening sun glittered off what looked like water through the brush. Could that be the tidal pool?

"There are mermaids in Talisman Lake?" Cori cried. "I learned to swim in that lake!"

"And you lived to tell the tale." I laughed to reassure her and checked the height of the fence to see if we could climb it, but it was about ten feet high and topped with a coil of barbed wire. "How big is this mall expansion going to be, anyway?"

Just then, a frighteningly loud rumble made us plaster ourselves against the fence as a large truck passed, followed by a huge cloud of dust. We coughed and waved our hands in front of our faces as it passed. The truck kept following the road for another hundred feet or so, then disappeared as someone swung open a large gate to let it through at the far end of the fencing.

"Come on!" I yelled. "That's got to be the way in."

We ran to the gate just as a beefy security guard clanged it shut and secured it with a large lock. He must not have noticed us, because he turned back to the orange and white construction trailer and started climbing the steps to go inside.

"Hey, wait!" I yelled, and coughed away the dirt cloud kicked up by the heavy truck.

The security guard paused at the top of the steps. "Can I help you?"

"We need to get in there!" I called.

"This is private property, miss," he answered. "Only authorized personnel allowed." He reached for the trailer door.

"Just a second!" I yelled. But what could I say? That my mermaid mother might be stuck in there? How was I supposed to wheedle my way into a locked construction area, skirted by a ten-foot barbed wire fence? And why such tight security, I wondered.

The security guard opened the trailer door midway. A television blared in the background. He turned to glare at me. "Look, all I want is to watch the last ten minutes of *Ultimate Survivor*, and for the last truckload of dirt to get here so I can finish my shift and go home. So whatever you want, make it quick."

"Uh." I looked to Luke, Trey, and Cori, but they shrugged hopelessly. I turned back to Grumpy McGrumpypants. "How much space is this mall expansion going to take, anyway?"

"The whole darn thing," the security guard answered, waving his arm back and forth to show that he meant everything. "They're putting in a new wing off Hyde's then landfilling the rest to plant some sort of urban garden or something. Now, unless you wanna get mowed over by a truck, I'd suggest you scram." He went into the trailer and slammed the door.

"The whole thing?" I whispered. I leaned on the fence next to Luke, wishing I could just walk through it, or under it or over it, but each option was as hopeless as the next.

"They're hiding something in there. I just know it," Luke said. "Why else would they have such tight security?"

Luke's phone rang. He stepped away to answer it, then put his hand over the receiver to talk to Trey. "It's Mrs. Clarke. She wants to know when we're going to go back to finish the raking."

Trey slapped his forehead. "Oh no. I completely forgot when you called me about the girl shorts." He put his hand out for the phone. "Here, let me talk to her."

"Hello, Mrs. Clarke?" Trey said. The rumble of a truck sounded in the distance. "Just a second, I'll move somewhere where I can hear you better." He covered his ear with his hand, and he and Luke moved down the road to try to sort out their lawn-mowing customer.

Cori and I sat on the rocks at the edge of the road by the ocean. "We need to get in there," I muttered.

"You really think your mom's in there?" Cori asked.

"I won't know until I can have a look," I replied.

"Wow." Cori shook her head in disbelief. "This is huge. I'm sorry I got mad at you back there, but I'm glad I finally know."

I put an arm around her shoulder. "Me too."

Just then, another truck filled with earth pulled up and stopped in front of the locked entry. It tooted its horn for someone to open the gate, but the security guard must have been busy catching the last few minutes of his show because he didn't come out of the trailer right away.

"Well, if we're gonna get in there, this is as good a

chance as any." Cori popped up from her seat on the rocks and ran to the back of the truck. She hopped onto the back bumper and grabbed the tailgate, turning toward me with her hand outstretched. "Come on!"

Chapter Nine

Y OU'RE CRAZY!" I LAUGHED and raced after Cori, jumping onto the truck just before it lurched forward and continued through the gate. Thankfully, the security guard was busy securing the lock as we entered the construction site and didn't turn our way before rushing back into his trailer to catch the last few minutes of his show.

Luke and Trey ran for the gate, laughing, and gave us a thumbs-up as the truck rolled away. I waved to them and flashed a hopeful smile, then grasped onto the tailgate to keep from becoming road pizza, hoping I didn't just make a huge mistake.

"This secret-identity stuff is fun!" Cori exclaimed, choking on the cloud of dust kicked up by the truck's massive back tires.

I put a finger to my lips to get her to shush. What would happen if we got caught? I seriously contemplated running back to the gate and waiting for the next truck to come through so we could escape. But then we turned a corner and I caught a glimpse of shimmering water through scrub brush and bushes, and any worries I may have had fell away.

"Oh wow."

"What?" Cori turned to see what I was "oh-wowing" about but the truck hit a pothole and she bounced off the bumper and onto the road.

"Cori!" The same weird superhuman (or super-mermish) force rose up inside of me like when she'd fallen into the ocean earlier, and suddenly I found myself leaping from the truck and shoulder rolling onto the gravel road to save her. "Oof!"

Okay. So maybe it wasn't the daintiest shoulder roll ever, but if my life ever became a blockbuster movie I promised myself I'd get a stunt double. I struggled to my feet and ran to Cori, just as she lifted her head. The truck rolled on down the road and around the bend, the driver oblivious, leaving us covered in dirt and coughing exhaust fumes.

I could hear another truck coming from the other way.

"Come on!" I propped Cori up and slung her arm over my shoulder. She stumbled as I dragged her off the road and into the bushes, out of the way of the oncoming truck. "Are you okay?"

"Yeah. I'll be fine." Cori rubbed her knee and turned back to the road. "Do you think anyone saw us?"

"Not sure, but let's not wait and find out. Are you okay to walk?"

"Lead the way, fish-girl." Cori raised her hand to point us onward.

We bushwhacked through the brush in the direction I'd

seen the water. After a few minutes, my flip-flops began to sink in the muck as the brush gave way to marshy grass and then open water about a hundred feet across.

"Could this be it?" I looked to my left in the direction of the ocean and saw the other end of the metal culvert jutting out into the pond. I had my answer. The culvert ran from the ocean to the pond, making it a tidal pool. Somewhere in there was my mother. I just knew it!

"Oh, hey! Take a picture, take a picture!" Cori tried to hand me her phone with one hand and held up her other arm where two Monarch butterflies had landed.

"Your phone went for a swim earlier, remember?" I laughed and rolled my eyes. "We could be arrested for breaking and entering and you want me to take a photo of butterflies?" Using my phone instead, I lined up the shot so I could get the butterflies on her arm and the dozen others flocking on a bunch of bushes nearby. I slipped my phone back in my pocket and looked out over the water.

"So do you think this is it?" Cori asked, touching one of the butterfly's wings before it flew away.

"I really hope so," I replied.

Sunlight glittered on the rippling waves of the pool, and all around it green shrubs waved in the summer breeze. A heron waded in the water not far from us but a loud clang set it off, just like it had earlier. I turned in the direction of the noise, and sure enough, up the hill closer to the mall, dump trunks unloaded earth while front-end loaders picked up a scoop at a time and dumped it into the north end of the pond. I worked my way through the bog to get to the open water but the mud was getting deeper and slowing me down.

"I can't believe they're just going to fill all this in," Cori said. "It's so pretty here…oooo…ouch!"

I turned to check on Cori and waited for her to catch up. "Are you sure you're okay?"

"Yeah." She limped toward me, grasping my arm for support, then shielded her eyes from the sun. "I'm good. Can you see anything?"

"Nothing. But I'm going to try to call out to her."

Cori glanced up the hill. "What if they hear you?"

"They won't hear me." I smiled.

Mom? I rang out over the water, hoping she'd hear.

"What was that?" Cori looked at me in amazement. "Was that you? Is that like mermaid Parseltongue or something?"

"Yeah. Sorta." I strained to hear in case Mom was trying to ring back but couldn't hear anything except a booming voice from behind us.

"Hey! You two!"

My heart seized in my chest.

"We are *so* dead." Cori tightened her grip on my arm and we turned slowly to face the guy who was probably about to bury us in the bog and make it look like an accident.

"I thought I told you kids to scram."

"Just thought we'd do a bit of bird watching?" I said hopefully.

Grumpy McGrumpypants looked at me sternly and

hitched up his leather utility belt which brimmed with brand-new looking survival gear. What exactly did he think he'd run up against in a field behind a shopping mall, I wondered. Killer turtles? Homicidal blue herons?

"I don't get paid enough for this," the security guard muttered, stomping toward us through the boggy muck.

"Oh yeah? Well, I know your employers personally." Cori put a hand on her hip. "And I doubt Mr. Chamberlain would appreciate the fact that you waste his money watching TV on company time."

"Whoa, now. Wait just a second." The security guard put up his hand. "No need to get all feisty." He turned from us and answered his ringing phone. "Yeah. I've got them here. The little one's giving me trouble but...uh, don't worry. I'll deal with it."

He eyed us and then continued his phone conversation.

I wasn't sure if "deal with it" meant fitting us with cement shoes, but any hope of finding Mom was slowly dwindling away. I turned back to the water, hoping for a sign before meeting my doom. And that's when I saw it.

An arm. Partway out of the water and only for a split second. Mom's arm? It had to be!

Mom! I rang.

The security guard put a hand over his ear like there was feedback from his phone but Cori looked at me, wide-eyed. And I must have actually jammed the phone's frequency because the security guard tapped it with the back of his hand.

"You still there?" he spoke into the mouthpiece. "Okay. Yeah, I can hear you again. Yeah, yeah, don't worry. I'll make sure they don't bother us again."

Cori's hand was beginning to cause deep tissue damage around my arm.

"Stay cool," I whispered.

But I was far from cool. All I wanted to do was crash through the bog and dive in the water after Mom, but with Grumpy McGrumpypants right there, that was definitely out of the question.

"Okay." The security guard clipped the phone back onto his belt and led us back to the road. "Here's what we're gonna do."

I turned back to see if I could catch one last glimpse of Mom but there was nothing. My chest filled with a rush of panic. Would I ever see her again? Could we stop the construction in time for her to make it back home safely?

Encouraged by the hand the security guard was keeping on his nightstick, we made it back to the road and kept walking to the chain-link gate. "You're gonna walk on out of here just like this never happened. Otherwise, I'll have the cops on you for trespassing like there's no tomorrow. *Capisce?*"

"Yup! We got it." Cori made a beeline for the gate, limping along on her bum leg.

"But Cori," I whispered, catching up to her, "my mom just waved to me back there."

"She did?" Cori replied as we spilled out to the road.

"What?" Luke asked. He and Trey rose from where they'd been sitting on the rocks at the side of the road to greet us. "What happened?"

"My mom is in the tidal pool. I saw her!" I looked back through the fence, desperate to run back into the construction site and fireman's carry her out of there. "We've got to do something."

"Well, we could tell that guy to tell his boss to stop piling rocks into the tidal pool because your mermaid mother is in the way, but I doubt that would help with the whole 'secret identity' thing." Cori nodded in the direction of the security guard as he swung the massive chain link gate closed.

"But…" My hands dropped to my sides. Cori was right.

"At least now we know where she is," Luke said quietly. "Didn't he say that was the last truck for the night?"

"Yes, but—"

"So, she'll be okay until the morning when we can figure something out." Luke put a hand on my shoulder and tried to catch my eye. "Okay?"

"Okay," I said, hearing the sound of metal on metal as the gate swung closed, just like the boat lock of Talisman Lake.

"Hey, fish-girl." Cori grabbed me by the arm and led me back up to the mall parking lot. "How about I buy you a Big Mac for your troubles? You know, for saving my life and all that?"

My stomach rumbled. I looked longingly at the golden arches off in the distance.

"That depends. Can I get fries with that?"

Chapter Ten

ORT TOULOUSE WASN'T GOING to win any awards for its wild and crazy night life. By the time we'd scarfed down our Super Value meals, the mall was closed and the buses had stopped running. I was bursting to tell Dad about what we'd found when I called to ask if he could pick us up, but the McDonald's was packed with screaming kids terrorizing the PlayPlace and I could barely hear him. Besides, I really wanted to see Dad's face when I delivered the news that we'd found Mom.

Luke and Trey were still waiting for their father when Dad arrived. His eyes scanned the booth, doing the mental calculations on our group.

"Hello…fellas." He nodded to Luke and Trey, then shuttled me and Cori to the car since Cori was coming over to my house to sleep over.

"You won't believe—" I began, but Dad interrupted me.

"You said you were going to McDonald's with Cori and 'the gang.'" Dad pulled onto the highway, stressing the last two words.

"Well, technically—" I glanced at Cori. Apparently, the trade-off for sleeping over was witnessing a lecture from my dad.

"Technically?" Dad interrupted me. "It may have been the nineteen hundreds when I was a teenager, but back in my day, two girls plus two boys was *technically* a double-date."

"It's not like that, we were just…" It was time to come clean before I got myself in even more trouble for stuff I didn't *actually* do. "We went looking for the tidal pool."

"Jade…" Dad looked from me to Cori in the rear-view mirror.

"Oh, don't worry, Mr. Baxter," Cori chimed in. "I know everything."

"Jade!" Dad cried.

"Dad, wait! I saw her! I saw Mom."

So, I spilled it all—Reese, Uncle Alzear, the culvert, and Renata. Then I explained about McDonald's and the construction site and the locked gate and seeing Mom's arm. Dad listened until we rumbled along the drawbridge, crossing over the canal.

"You saw her?" he said. "Was she okay?"

"I couldn't tell. The security guard almost called the cops on us before he kicked us out."

"The cops? Jade! This is exactly the kind of thing I was afraid of."

"But she was there, Dad. We actually found her."

"And I am *thrilled* you've found your mom." I could see Dad blink a few times in the rearview mirror. "But I am less than thrilled with the fact that you risked your life and almost got arrested in the process. Why didn't you call me right away when you first met Reese?"

"I dunno."

"Honestly, Jade. We talked about this!"

Cori gave me an understanding smile. Despite getting reamed out by Dad, one thing was for sure: it was a relief to finally have her in on my secret.

"It's just…" I looked past the railing to the dark waters of Talisman Lake where my mermaid journey had begun just a few short weeks before. "We've been disappointed so many times. I just wanted to make sure."

Thankfully, Dad didn't continue to freak out on me just then, but I think I had Cori's presence to thank for that. When we got home and Cori ducked into the bathroom, though, Dad obviously had a little time to think about what he had to say.

"You have *got* to stop doing this." Dad rested his hands on my shoulders as we stood in our front hall. "How can I trust you if you keep shutting me out? We're supposed to be a team, remember?"

It was true. I *had* gone behind his back. And if I ever hoped to leave the house again, I'd have to grovel like a prairie dog.

"I know. I'm really sorry, Dad. It was thoughtless and reckless and I'm a horrible, horrible daughter." I finished off my groveling with a goofy grin and jazz hands to help lighten the mood. "But ta-da! I still found Mom."

Dad couldn't hide his smile. "A horrible daughter who is growing up horribly fast."

"So, do you forgive me?" I asked.

"I'll think about it." Dad gave me a hug. "Right now, I am going to go upstairs to the computer to try and figure out what's going on with this mall construction business. Try not to put your life in mortal peril in the meantime?"

"I'll do my best," I replied.

Cori pelted me with mermaid-related trivia questions while we watched music videos on YouTube and raided the kitchen for snacks.

"So, what happens to your legs when you grow a tail? Like where do they go?" she asked.

"I dunno. It happens so fast it's kind of like an explosion. Growing legs is a bit slower and a lot more painful."

"Like burning-your-neck-with-a-hair-straightener painful or plucking-your-eyebrows-with-a-pair-of-tweezers painful? Cause one is more of a searing pain and the other is more of a sharp, stabbing pain, I think."

Where did she get this stuff?

"I'd have to go with hair-straightener option if I had to choose," I answered.

Grocery shopping wasn't really my dad's specialty, so it was slim pickings in the kitchen unless you wanted Sugar-O cereal, two week-old Wonder bread, or soy sauce.

"You got any popcorn?" Cori searched in the cupboard over the fridge. "Ah, here."

Cori plucked an Orville Redenbacher box from the shelf but shook it upside down to show it was empty. I stashed the box in the overflowing recycle bin underneath the kitchen sink.

"Sorry. We might have some leftover kernels from that time we made popcorn cranberry garlands with my grandmother at Christmas. We don't have a popper, though."

"No biggie." Cori found a paper lunch bag in one of the kitchen cupboards. She measured the leftover popcorn before pouring it inside, then stapled the bag shut.

"Are you going to put that in the microwave like that?" I asked, worried that we were going to get electrocuted from the metal on the staples.

"Trust me, I Googled it." Cori set the microwave to Popcorn and pressed Enter just as the song on YouTube ended. "Oh! Did you see the video of Chelse yet?"

"Is it really bad?" It felt a little wrong wanting to look, but Cori had the video cued up on Facebook before I had a chance to say no.

The video started off with Chelse walking along the dock at her family's cottage near my Gran's in Dundee. She had her head down, texting someone on her phone while her dog ran around her, barking at something in the water. The video maker had added really bad, super dorky pop music and text message captions at the bottom of the screen.

gurl1: hey gurl!
gurl2: hey gurl! whatcha doing?

gurl1: i dunno. whatcha doing?

gurl2: i dunno…just texting you. whatcha doing?

Just then, the dog ran in front of Chelse and she wiped out and fell in the water, phone in hand.

I'm not proud of it, but I stifled a laugh.

"I know, right?" Cori said. "Looks like someone else we know, huh?"

"I think your splash was bigger," I teased, remembering Cori's swan dive into the Atlantic Ocean earlier that day.

At the end of the video, Chelse flailed in the water, holding her phone overhead and a final message crossed the screen.

WARNING: Friends don't let friends walk and text.

"It has 1,584 likes and 374 comments?" I stared at the view counter. "No wonder Chelse was upset. This thing is spreading like crazy."

"It's all over Facebook." Cori plopped a glob of butter into a measuring cup then found brown sugar, salt, and chocolate chips, and mixed it all into a gooey buttery concoction while the popcorn finished popping.

"I feel kinda bad for watching it," I admitted, shutting the laptop.

"Yeah." Cori looked at me and cringed. "After doing the same thing at Toulouse Point, now I kind of do too."

The timer dinged, so I pulled out the steaming bag

of popcorn so Cori could put her buttery mixture in the microwave to melt.

"Sorry," I said. "This is the lamest sleepover ever. First you have to listen to a lecture from my dad, then you have to make your own snacks. At least when my mom was here we had a better stocked kitchen."

"Yeah, about that. How exactly are you going to explain your mom's sudden reappearance when she makes it back home?"

"*If* she makes it back home." I pulled down a bowl from the cupboard and set it on the counter, then ripped open the paper bag to pour the popcorn into it.

"She's *totally* going to make it back."

"Thanks, Cori." I smiled, relieved to know I had a few extra people on my side now compared to my lone-girl rescue mission when I helped my mom escape Talisman Lake a few weeks before. "You're awesome."

"So I've been told. But you wanna know what else is awesome?" Cori poured the steaming mixture of butter, salt, sugar, and chocolate over the bowl of popcorn, and tossed it all together. "This popcorn."

She held out the bowl for me.

"Don't mind if I do," I replied.

Chapter Eleven

CORI WAS SNORING BY the time Dad came by to check on me. A quick glance at my alarm clock told me it was nearly 1 a.m.

"Sleeping?" Dad asked quietly. He collapsed into the wicker chair beside my bed and rubbed his hands over his face.

"Not really." I turned over, yanking the blankets back from Cori since she'd wrapped herself up like a mummy. Total blanket hog. Cori grunted something about razor clams and circus clowns and went back to her snoring. "What did you find out?"

"Thankfully, civic bylaws don't allow construction in public places on the weekends, so your mom should be safe until Monday, at least. Maybe we can figure out how to get in there in the meantime."

"Good luck with that," I said, rubbing my eyes. "Did you know there's a ten-foot barbed-wire fence surrounding the tidal pool? Luke thinks they're hiding something."

"Yeah, about Luke." Dad paused for a second. "He is, um, just a friend, right?"

"Well." I wasn't sure what to say. Was Luke more than just a friend? He was my first kiss but that was over three weeks ago. He'd held my hand today but said what he really needed was a friend who understood him.

"Because I'm not sure if I'm okay with my little girl dating." Dad stood and paced a bit but bumped into my dresser in the dark and stubbed his toe. "Oh, ouch."

"Wha...?" Cori sat up in bed and waved her head back and forth, her eyes still closed. "Is the clam in the bucket? Did the clown put the clam in the bucket?" she babbled.

"Go back to sleep, Cori," I said quietly.

She lay back down and kept snoring.

"I'm not exactly a little girl anymore, Dad. Lots of girls date at fourteen."

"What are you saying? When did you go on a date with this boy? Why don't I know anything about this?" Dad asked.

"It wasn't a date, exactly. We just—well, we kissed that one time, but that doesn't mean—"

"You kissed?" Dad's "whisper" was loud enough to wake the neighbors, but Cori slept on, oblivious. He paced back and forth at the end of my bed, rubbing his head as he walked. "No, no, no. I am not comfortable with this. There's lots of time for that. *Lots* of time."

That's when I started getting mad. Here I was pretty much taking care of myself ever since Mom disappeared the summer before. I was a model student (except for last term), a model daughter (if you didn't look at the mess under my bed), and pretty much cooked every meal we ate in this house (my Hot Pockets were especially delicious). Where did Dad get off saying I wasn't mature enough to date? That was what he was saying, wasn't it?

"Are you telling me I *can't* date?" I asked.

Dad sat back down and shook his head hopelessly. "I'd just rather you wait. Yes. Just wait until your mom gets home."

"But—"

Dad stood and made his getaway before I could say anything. Last time I saw him move that fast, he was being chased by a cloud of wasps.

Cori sat at a stool at the kitchen island the next morning, sprawled across the countertop. I poured her a glass of orange juice and placed it in front of her. She flashed me a peace sign without looking up.

I grabbed a bag of peas from the freezer and held it out for her. "Here, put this on your knee."

"I'll be fine," Cori mumbled, but her knee was swollen to the size of a small watermelon from jumping off the construction truck and she could barely walk. I dropped the bag of frozen peas in her lap anyway. "Oh geesh! That's cold!" she cried.

"That's the point," I teased and pointed to her leg. "Twenty minutes!"

"All right, all right!" Cori placed the peas on her knee. "When did you get so bossy?"

"Just giving you a taste of your own medicine." I poured some Sugar-Os in a couple bowls and got the milk from the fridge.

Just then, Dad came into the kitchen to refill his cup of coffee. "Good morning, ladies."

"Good morning, Mr. B.," Cori said.

"What's with the peas?" he asked.

"My knee's just a little stiff. It'll be fine once I get to work," Cori said.

Dad looked from Cori to me. "Oh, no. You shouldn't go to work with an injury like that. Jade would be happy to do your shift today since you filled in for her yesterday afternoon, wouldn't you, Jade?"

"But—" I began. The last thing I wanted to do was spend the day scooping ice cream when Mom was floating in a tidal pool behind Port Toulouse Mall, but the look on Dad's face suggested I didn't have much of a choice in the matter. "Of course. I'll take your shift, Cori."

"You sure?" Cori raised her head from the counter.

"I'm sure. It's the *mature* thing to do." I eyed Dad, making sure he caught my drift from the conversation we'd had the night before.

"Cool." Cori flopped back onto the counter and closed her eyes.

"Jade." Dad sighed as he poured a bit of milk in his coffee. "I know you're not happy with how we left things last night."

"You mean the part about how I'm not allowed to

date?" I grabbed a couple spoons from the cutlery drawer and jabbed them into each bowl, spilling a bit of the milk in the process.

"I'd just feel better if you waited until your mom was here to walk you through this dating thing, that's all. Besides, you seem to forget how I made a total fool of myself with that other thing." He said "thing" between clenched teeth like he'd rather forget our feminine hygiene–product shopping trip from back in June.

"You weren't that bad," I said but cringed at the memory.

"Still, I'm sure your mom would be much better qualified to deal with this." He stirred his coffee then tapped the spoon on the side of his mug. "You get it, don't you?"

"Sure," I said vaguely. "I get it."

"Thanks, honey." He smiled as he picked up his coffee mug and headed back up to the office upstairs.

"I get that I'm going to grow up to be an old maid living alone with twenty-nine cats if my dad has anything to do with it," I muttered as I heard Dad's footsteps on the stairs.

"Cats? Wha…what cats?" Cori sat up, confused.

"Never mind, just eat up." I placed a bowl of cereal in front of her and popped a spoonful of Sugar-Os in my mouth.

Someone knocked on the kitchen door.

"Hi, Mrs. Blake," I said as I opened the door. Cori's mom had come to pick her up.

"Hello, sweetness." Mrs. Blake gave me a hug and a

peck on the cheek. She handed me a still-warm, home-baked lasagna and a basketful of peaches. "Did you girls have fun?"

"Yes, but wow." I peeked under the aluminum foil and snuck a piece of cheesy pasta. "You didn't have to do this."

"Don't be silly." Mrs. Blake waved my comment away. "It's just as easy to make two lasagnas as it is to make one, and they were practically giving the peaches away at the farmer's market."

I polished off the rest of my Sugar-Os and rinsed out my bowl before serving myself a piece of lasagna as big as my head.

"Ohmygarmmm. This is so goorf," I said as I chewed, imagining the day when my own mom would be standing in the kitchen making me food.

"Glad you like it." Mrs. Blake squeezed my arm and smiled. "Cori, honey. Are you almost ready to go? What happened to your knee?"

"I twisted it." Cori winced as she propped her leg up on the stool next to her. "Which totally stinks. How am I supposed to go to the movie tonight like this?"

"And with whom were you planning to go to the movie?" Mrs. Blake raised her eyebrows.

"With Trey," Cori began, then she saw the skeptical look on her mother's face, "and Jade, and maybe Luke? There's a big group of us, I think."

Dad had left things a bit fuzzy. Was going to the movies

in a group okay, or was my social life doomed for the foreseeable future?

Mrs. Blake pursed her lips and looked back and forth between the two of us.

"Can't wait!" I exclaimed, maybe a bit too cheerily but I couldn't leave Cori hanging.

"As long as there's a group," Mrs. Blake said. "You know how I feel about you dating. Trey Martin seems like a nice boy but he *is* almost sixteen."

An icy silence filled the room. Cori shifted the bag of peas on her knee.

"Well, look at the time!" I glanced at the clock on the microwave. "If I'm going to take over your scooping duties today, we all better get going."

"I'll give you a ride over." Mrs. Blake popped the rest of the lasagna in the fridge and picked up her purse. "Grab your things and meet me in the car when you're ready?"

"Sure. Thanks!"

Mrs. Blake left through the kitchen door while Cori dug around her cereal.

"Can you believe that?" Cori picked up her bowl and limped over to the sink. "It's SO unfair."

I thought back to the conversation I'd just had with my dad.

"I feel your pain, my friend. I really do," I mumbled as I finished up my last bite of lasagna. "Add scales and a tail and we're practically the same person."

Chapter Twelve

"CHELSE?" I CALLED. MELTING ice cream dripped down my hand as I handed a triple order of chocolate dipped soft-serve over the counter to the waiting customers. They waved their money for me to take, but I was way too sticky.

"Chelse, honey." Bridget nudged her as she headed out into the diner with a club sandwich platter and a plate of calamari.

Finally, Chelse pulled out her earbuds and glanced up from her cell phone.

I turned back and smiled at the customer. "Chelse can help you at the end of the counter."

"Oh, sorry." Chelse blinked and took the money from the customer and actually made the right amount of change as far as I could tell.

Once the customers were gone, I turned to wash my hands in the sink, then leaned back against the counter to dry them with a paper towel. Chelse looked so sad. Sure, I was peeved because I pretty much had to carry the shift on my own whenever I worked with her (plus all of my earnings were still getting socked away until I could figure out how to pay for the canoe of hers I'd lost), but I couldn't help feel bad for her. And guilty.

"Hey, Chelse?" I asked. "You okay?"

Chelse looked up at me. Her face drooped in its usual cheerless expression, but then she forced a smile. "Yeah. I'm fine."

"Anything you want to talk about?" I asked. "I'm a good listener."

Chelse glanced out our awning-covered window to check for customers, then sat back on her stool in front of the till.

"So, I guess you heard about the Facebook thing?"

I nodded and gave an embarrassed smile.

"I'm sure that can't be fun for you. I'm sorry." I suddenly felt *really* bad for watching the video in the first place. How embarrassing would it be to have something like that splashed all over the Internet?

And there I was, watching the video just like the other 374 dopes who'd thought it would be funny to make stupid jokes in the comments. Did those people even know Chelse? Did they even care? And what did that make *me* if I couldn't resist the temptation to have a look too?

"Yeah, well. First of all, my boyfriend promised me he'd deleted that video like I'd asked." Chelse squinted, as if remembering something, and shook her head. "But after we broke up, he thought he'd have fun with it and post it all over Facebook. A couple hundred mouse clicks later, here we are." She stuffed her phone into her purse and folded her hands in her lap.

"Your ex-boyfriend did this to you?" I stared at her in surprise. "What an idiot."

"Wow." Chelse laughed. "Thanks. You're the first person to actually talk to me about it."

"No problem," I said.

"The video *was* kind of funny, though," Chelse said quietly. A smile crept over her lips.

"And I see Buster is just as hyper as ever," I joked, thinking back to all the fun we used to have when I visited my Gran's cottage across the water from the Beckers'. "Remember when we tried to teach him how to water-ski that time?"

Chelse laughed. "And he kept licking the water, then he puked all over your Gran's dock."

"Yeah and then my mom stepped in it before we could clean it up?"

Chelse was giggling like crazy by then.

"Sorry!" She held a hand to her mouth. "I shouldn't be laughing."

"Why not?" I smiled. "It *was* pretty hilarious."

Chelse wiped the laughter tears from her eyes. "Your mom was so much fun. It's been weird not seeing her this summer."

"Yeah, she was," I agreed, remembering our summers in Dundee. "Anyway, about the video? Forget about it and that loser ex-boyfriend of yours. I can't believe anyone would want to hurt you like that."

Chelse looked down at her hands like she was missing something now that her cell was stowed away in the bag under her stool.

"Thanks, Jade. The problem is…I'm not the only one who could get hurt by this," she said quietly.

I wasn't sure I'd heard her correctly, but just then Bridget came by to fill in for my break.

"Made you some fries. Extra salty." She motioned to the counter where a huge plate of waffle fries sat waiting.

"Bridget, did I ever tell you I love you more than puppies and rainbows? Because I do." I hugged her and went around the counter, parking myself on the swivel stool in front of my plate of fries. My mouth watered in anticipation for the salty, starchy goodness, but I restrained myself and called Dad to get an update.

"Hey, Dad. How's it going?" I asked when he picked up the phone.

"Jade! I'm so glad you called. I made a few inquiries about the construction site and found out a few interesting things."

"Like what?" I looked around to make sure no one was listening.

"Apparently, Chamberlain Construction has special permission from the Land Development Department to work over the weekends," Dad said.

"You mean they're landfilling at the mall right now?" Panic rose in my chest. "How can they do that?"

Dad paused. "I get the feeling Mr. Chamberlain is a well-connected man."

"We've got to do something." I could feel the tears gathering up in the corners of my eyes. "What if—"

But I stopped myself when I saw Bridget look up from scooping up a banana split. She quickly turned away when her customer asked for extra peanuts.

"I'm working on something right now. We'll talk about it when you get home, okay?" Dad said.

"Okay," I whispered before saying good-bye.

Bridget tended to the coffee pot while there was a lull at the ice cream counter. She stopped when she saw I hadn't touched my fries yet.

"Too salty?" she asked.

"Oh." I looked down at my plate and popped a fry in my mouth. "No, no. They're perfect."

Bridget paused. "I couldn't help but overhear. Are they expanding the mall? I haven't been shopping there since the spring."

"Yeah. They're putting in a new wing and landfilling the back part by the shore." I looked down at my plate imagining each load of dirt going into the tidal pool. What would happen to Mom if we didn't get to her on time?

Chelse called over from her perch. "Is that what all those trucks are for? I could barely find a parking spot last time I was there."

"It's too bad they're filling all that in." Bridget poured

the old coffee in the sink and began to make a fresh pot. "It's really pretty back there with the pond and everything."

"You know where I mean?" I asked. My eyes stung. I wiped a tear away.

"Yeah. Hey." Bridget reached out and touched my arm. Chelse looked over from the ice cream counter. "What's the matter?"

"It's just…" How could I explain why I was so upset without revealing the fact that Mom was floating in the mall's tidal pool? "That place is—*was*—really special to my mom."

"It *is* pretty special," Bridget said thoughtfully. "Especially when the Monarch butterflies are migrating."

"Oh, I have a picture of that." I scrolled through the pictures on my phone to find the one of Cori from the day before. I held it up for her to see. Bridget smiled as if remembering a similar time.

"How can they just landfill a place like that?" Chelse took my phone in her hands and studied the picture.

"Well, they shouldn't *really*," Bridget said slowly. "Considering."

"Considering what?" A hopeful feeling rose in my chest.

"Monarchs are a 'species of special concern.'" Bridget finger-quoted the last bit. "Kind of one step away from being endangered."

"I didn't know you were such a nature lover," Chelse said.

"Kind of a sucker for a good cause, more like." Bridget pressed the button on the coffee maker and wiped down the counter with a cloth. "I actually tried to get that area protected by the town a few years ago."

"What happened?" I tried to keep cool, but the possibility of protecting the tidal pool somehow was the first glimmer of hope I'd had all day.

"I couldn't get enough people behind it." Bridget rinsed her cloth in the sink and hung it to dry over the faucet.

I sighed, unable to hide my disappointment.

Chelse looked from me to Bridget, a look of disgust on her face.

"Are you kidding me?" Chelse asked. "Over a thousand people will watch a stupid video on Facebook but you couldn't get enough people to speak up for an almost-endangered species? What is *wrong* with people?" Then a smile grew on her lips. "Or maybe…"

"What?" I looked from Bridget to Chelse. "Maybe what?"

Chelse pulled out her phone.

"I'm friending you on Facebook. Send me that picture?" She nodded to the picture of Cori with the butterflies.

"Sure, but what are you going to do with it?"

"I'm going to attempt to restore my faith in humanity."

Chapter Thirteen

B Y DINNERTIME, CHELSE HAD set up a Facebook page and had 37 likes. Dad was reheating Mrs. Blake's lasagna in the microwave while I filled Cori in on the news over the phone.

"Butterflies versus Boutiques." I read the title of the Facebook page as I surfed the web at the kitchen counter.

"She used my butterfly arm. Cool!" Cori said.

Chelse had cropped the picture from my cell phone to show just Cori's arm and a dump truck off in the distance. In the description she'd written, "Mall construction is destroying Monarch butterfly habitat. Join our protest to save this beautiful butterfly from becoming endangered."

"Do you think it'll work?" Cori asked.

"Not sure." I scrolled through the page's members but only recognized a few people. Some wondered what the group was all about. Some agreed with how wrong it was to destroy Monarch butterfly habitat for the sake of a larger mall. Others posted pictures of their cats.

"Guess it can't hurt," Cori said. "I'm going to share the link with my friends."

I clicked the Share button and did the same. Not that I thought my 258 friends would make much of a difference, but by the time I returned to the Butterflies vs. Boutiques page, seven more people had joined.

I clicked on Chelse's profile. "Chelse is popular, huh? Over a thousand friends."

"Oh wow," Cori said.

"What?" I asked.

"Did you see what she just put on her wall?"

"No. What?" I refreshed Chelse's page but it took forever to reload on my decrepit laptop. "Oh!"

I know you're all wondering about THE VIDEO! :) Watch it on the Butterflies vs. Boutiques page and while you're there, help support a good friend, a great listener, and a worthy cause.

I clicked back to the Butterflies vs. Boutiques page. Chelse had posted a video with the caption "New and Improved!"

"What does 'New and Improved' mean?" I asked.

"Shh…I'm watching it now," Cori said.

I pressed Play and waited for the video to buffer. It was the same video her ex-boyfriend had posted but with new captions.

gurl1: hey gurl!
gurl2: hey gurl! whatcha doing?

gurl1: figuring out that my ex-boyfriend is a moron. whatcha doing?

gurl2: agreeing with you.

The dog ran in front of Chelse and made her trip, just as before, but this time the video stopped while she was in midair. A new caption flashed at the end.

WARNING: Don't fall for morons because they might put stupid videos of you on Facebook.

"Oh, ha-ha! That's awesome," I said.

"I know, right?" Cori replied.

"What's this?" Dad leaned across the counter to see. He placed a bowl of steaming lasagna in front of me.

"Call you later," I said before hanging up.

"This is what you were saying earlier?" Dad scrolled through the page. "About the Monarch butterfly?"

"Yeah. We've already got"—I refreshed the page and felt a rush of excitement—"154 likes! Cool, right?"

"I dunno, Jade. Do you really think a *Facebook* page is going to do any good?"

A roiling anger boiled up inside of me. Here we were, trying to do something to make a difference (well, actually it was Chelse's idea, but whatever), and our parents *still* didn't take us seriously. "Do you have any better ideas?"

"As a matter of fact, I do. Eddie and I are going to work

on the Merlin 3000 tonight." Dad bobbed his eyebrows then dug into his bowl of lasagna.

If they got the Merlin 3000 up and running and *if* we could somehow get to mom, then it wouldn't matter if she had finished her transformation yet. That was more *ifs* than I was comfortable with.

The doorbell rang as I glanced at the Facebook page again. 247 likes.

"Oh good. Gran's here." Dad went to the front hall to answer the door.

"Gran?" I stabbed my fork into my lasagna. Not only was I not allowed to date but now I needed a baby-sitter?

I guess going to the movies was out of the question.

With Dad and Eddie playing mad scientist, there was nothing left to do but watch TV bingo with Gran, surf the net, and worry and wait.

Gran sat on the couch next to me with two TV tray tables full of bingo cards. Her hands were a bingo dabbing blur, marking each number as the local cable announcer called out the numbers.

"I'm honored you gave up your Sunday Roulette Night at the casino to hang out with me," I kidded.

"Oh, not roulette, silly. Sunday night is half-price slots." She slapped my knee and squeezed it with a giggle, never missing a bingo number in the process. "But anything for my little Jadie."

I had to admit, it didn't feel quite as condescending

when Gran called me little. She was my grandmother, after all. So maybe she wasn't a typical grandma, but at least she had an excuse for talking to me like a six-year-old.

"Watch my cards while I go to the little girls' room, will you, Jadie?" Gran got up and adjusted her *Embrace Your Inner Cheesecake* T-shirt around her wide hips. "Otherwise, I'll have to rip a toot and it won't be pretty."

Like I said: not typical.

"Got you covered." I put my laptop on the side table next to the couch and grabbed her bingo marker to start dabbing dots over all her N-42s. Gah! She had a *lot* of cards.

The phone rang.

I fumbled to answer it while trying to listen to the announcer call the next number.

"Hey," Cori said.

"Hi. You got my text? Sorry about the movie."

"No worries. My knee is still killing me and my mom wasn't too keen on the idea anyway. That's not why I called. Did you see the invitation?"

"What invitation?" I asked.

"B-7," the TV announcer called.

"Check Facebook," Cori replied.

I dabbed as many B-7s as I could find then refreshed the screen on the Butterflies vs. Boutiques Facebook page. We were up to 473 members and Chelse had created an event and invited everyone to attend.

BUTTERFLIES vs. BOUTIQUES RALLY

"What's this all about?" I asked.

"Chelse is trying to get a bunch of people together for a protest," Cori said.

"O-72," the announcer called out from the TV.

"Just a sec." I scanned Gran's cards to find all her O-72s.

"What the heck are you doing, anyway?" Cori asked.

"You don't want to know." I laughed.

Thankfully, Gran got back from her washroom break and shooed me away so she could take over bingo duty. I scooted over to the side of the couch with my laptop to have a better look at the invitation.

Time: Monday, August 1, 10:00 a.m.

Location: Port Toulouse Mall

Created by: BUTTERFLY vs. BOUTIQUES

More Info: Chamberlain Construction says they are a GREEN company, but their Port Toulouse Mall expansion is threatening the Monarch butterfly's precious habitat. Wear GREEN to help stop the Port Toulouse mall construction. Do your part to save this special species.

"This is for tomorrow?" I asked.

"Yeah, but I can't go because I have to work, which totally bites," Cori said.

I scanned the invitation again. "Chelse really has taken this butterfly idea and run with it, huh?"

"No kidding."

"Oh, what the heck, it can't hurt." I accepted the invitation, but almost wished I hadn't since the only people who'd confirmed were Chelse, Trey, Luke, and me. I hated to admit it, but maybe Dad was right. Did this Facebook thing stand a chance?

"Oh! BINGO!!" Gran called out, nearly making me fall off the couch. "Bingo! Bingo! Get off the phone, Jadie. I need to call it in!"

"Sorry, Cori! Gotta go!" I hung up so Gran could call the TV station to claim her prize and stared at the four lonely profile pictures in the rally's Attending column. Would tomorrow's rally help save my mom or just be another huge disappointment?

Chapter Fourteen

F OUR KIDS WEARING GREEN T-shirts in front of a mall didn't exactly qualify as a rally. People kept handing us their shopping carts to take them back into Hyde's Department Store, mistaking us for parking lot attendants. One asked Luke and Trey if their Boy Scout troop was collecting donations for the Food Bank.

The chances of stopping the mall construction and saving Mom were not looking good.

"We should get ready. It's almost ten." Chelse handed me a pair of dollar-store butterfly wings. "Here, I brought extras."

"Thanks!" I said. Chelse had worked so hard, making signs, setting up the Facebook page—everything—to help protect the Monarch. Little did she know she might be helping another endangered species too: Mers. "My mom would really appreciate all this."

"Don't mention it. It's for a good cause." Chelse grinned a mischievous smile. "Plus, my video has almost as many views as my ex-boyfriend's. My faith in humanity has been restored."

I laughed. "Yeah, well, you're making a difference."

How *much* of a difference, I wasn't sure, since just then a dump truck rumbled up the gravel road behind McDonald's. I shivered at the thought of Mom getting buried under one of those piles of dirt and turned to Trey and Luke while Chelse checked her phone.

"The trucks have been streaming in and out of the construction site ever since we got here." Dread sat in my belly like a heavy stone. "Do you guys know if anyone else is coming?"

Trey and Luke looked at each other for a brief second and Luke let out a little laugh.

"What? Didn't *anybody* else sign up?" I asked.

Luke pointed out to the parking lot and smiled. "See for yourself."

I looked out at all the parked cars and didn't understand what he meant at first. Then, people in green T-shirts began to get out of cars and trucks, come out of the McDonald's, disembark from a huge yellow bus with the words CAMP WHYCOCOMAGH written across the side, and make their way toward us through the parking lot.

"Green means green! Green means green!"

There were dozens at first, then many, many dozens, and soon after, a sea of green appeared.

"Butterflies not Boutiques! Butterflies not Boutiques!"

"Wow. These people are all for the rally?" I asked in disbelief.

"That or they were having a sale on green T-shirts at Hyde's." Luke handed me a sign and smiled.

"Over here!" I yelled, waving the sign high into the air

so the crowd could see us. There was "butterscotch sundae" Maeve from the post office, "banana-split" sharing Mr. and Mrs. Howser, and the lady with baby Olivia and the gelato-loving little boy, plus many, many more.

It took me about three seconds to turn into a blubbering, snot-bubble crybaby, but I didn't care. I just couldn't believe how many people had actually showed up.

"Thanks so much for coming!" I said to each person I greeted, handing them a pamphlet.

Pretty awesome, huh? Luke leaned over and rang into my ear.

More than awesome. I just hope it's enough, I replied.

"Hey, you got a pair of wings for us?" A voice from behind made me jump. I turned.

"Cori!" I hugged her tightly. "I thought you had to work!"

"Well, there's *nobody* on Main Street, so the boss figured we should close up shop and join in on the fun." Cori stepped to the side to reveal Bridget popping open a humongous cooler of ice cream.

"Wow, guys!" I fought back more tears. "I just don't know what to say. Thank you. This is all so awesome. How's your knee?" I asked Cori.

"Better. Plus, there was no way I was going to miss this!" she replied.

"Green means green! Green means green!" the crowd chanted. "Butterflies not Boutiques! Butterflies not Boutiques!"

But despite all our banner waving and chanting, the trucks kept rolling up and down the gravel construction road.

Any one of those loads of earth could be burying my mom right now, I rang to Luke.

Well, then. Let's take this show on the road. Luke whistled to Trey who was directing traffic in the parking lot. He pointed to the truck kicking up a cloud of dirt along the road.

Trey understood and leaned in to talk to a group of tattooed motorcyclists that had just driven up. The leader of the pack smiled and nodded his head for his pals to follow, then wheeled his bike through the parking lot to the gravel road, which they parked across.

"Hey! This way!" Luke waved for everyone to follow him.

Cori and Chelse grabbed the ice cream cooler while I carried the extra signs and butterfly wings. We looked like a humongous green snake as our rally weaved through the parking lot to join the motorcycle blockade.

"Oh. Wait a second!" I rushed over to the biggest biker and handed him a pair of purple sparkly wings. He chuckled and slipped the elastic straps around his muscular shoulders. His buddy flipped one of his wings and laughed, but butterfly biker swatted his hand away.

A dump truck exited the highway and slowed down as it approached the crowd. The driver blared his horn for the motorcycles to move, but the tattooed, leather-vested bikers leaned back on their bike seats and folded their beefy, tanned arms across their chests.

The truck driver opened his door and scanned the crowd. "Butterflies not boutiques!"

He shook his head and sat back in his truck.

"Green means green!"

"How many people signed up for this, anyway?" I asked Luke once he finally made his way through the crowd to me. The crowd's chants were so loud I could barely hear myself speak.

Luke got his phone out and searched for the Facebook invitation. "Lots!"

There *were* lots—352 to be exact. They kept arriving in cars and buses while others came out of the mall to see what our protest was all about. In fact, one of the most recent arrivals was making a beeline for our group.

"Lainey Chamberlain." Cori stepped in front of her. "I see you got my invitation."

"What exactly do you think you're doing?" Lainey's perfectly straightened hair skimmed her shoulders as she glanced around the crowd.

Cori handed her a pamphlet. "Stopping your daddy's mall construction. And saving the Monarch butterfly."

"Oh really?" Lainey ignored the pamphlet and looked up to the sky and smiled. "Well, we'll just see about that."

Seconds later, the *whomp, whomp, whomp* of something big and ominous sounded from above.

"A helicopter?" Trey called out over the noise. "Cool!"

"Not cool!" I cried. Especially when the sound of sirens filled the air as a police car pulled up from the direction of the highway and a security car screeched to a halt on the other side of our group, from the construction side.

"Wow!" Bridget shouted. "You kids definitely know how to get people's attention."

"Must be the ice cream!" Cori handed out two more cones to the gathering crowd.

The helicopter did a flyby of our crowd, then landed in an empty field a couple hundred feet away. A tall, tanned man who looked like he'd just stepped off the golf course emerged from the helicopter's side door flanked by two business-suited pinheads carrying briefcases.

"Daddy!" Lainey rushed over to greet him and held out her arms for a hug, but Mr. Chamberlain didn't seem to notice her.

"Get the lawyers on this," he boomed to the pinhead on his right as the helicopter propellers whirred to a stop. He scanned the crowd and scowled. "*Now!*"

"Daddy," Lainey tried again.

Mr. Chamberlain stopped short and took off his sunglasses.

"Lainey?" he asked. "What are you doing here?"

Lainey rubbed her arms as if a cold breeze had just swept over her.

"I'm the one who called your office earlier. They're trying to stop your mall project." She handed him the pamphlet. He scanned it quickly, then gave it back with a wave of his hand.

"Darling, this doesn't concern you." Mr. Chamberlain put his sunglasses back on and stalked over to the police car. Lainey followed him. She looked down at the pamphlet and unfolded it as she went.

"What are we supposed to do now?" I asked once Lainey and her dad were out of earshot.

"Yeah, Mr. Chamberlain doesn't exactly look like the bargaining type." Cori watched as he gestured toward the crowd while talking to the police.

I dropped my sign to my side and turned to Luke. *Any ideas?*

Just wait a sec. Luke scrolled through something on his phone. "Someone posted a link on our Facebook page about a subway line that had to be totally rerouted because of a rare kind of tree."

Luke handed me his phone just as the policeman turned on the siren and lights.

"Attention, everyone!" the policeman called out through his bullhorn. "You are welcome to continue your demonstration, but you need to clear this road." He swept his arm over the crowd, motioning to the edges of the road. A few moms with strollers pushed them onto the grassy area.

"Daddy?" Lainey said as Mr. Chamberlain made his way back to his waiting helicopter. She held up the pamphlet. "Is this true? Is the construction destroying the Monarch's habitat?"

Something on Luke's phone screen caught my eye—one detail that could change everything. Could it be? Could this be the thing that would stop Chamberlain Construction in its tracks?

I rushed after Lainey and her dad, trying to read the information on the phone's screen while Mr. Chamberlain stalked back to his helicopter followed by his pinheads. He turned to face his daughter before climbing in.

"Don't believe everything you read, darling. These people are menaces, keeping people from doing their jobs," he said, scanning the crowd. "This is a multimillion-dollar project and idle trucks cost me money."

Mr. Chamberlain pointed to the two dump trucks parked along the road waiting to get through as the crowd moved to the side.

"Green means green!"

"Butterflies not boutiques!"

Finally, I had what I wanted. I looked up from Luke's cell phone. "Mr. Chamberlain?"

"I've got to get back to my golf game, sweetie," he said to Lainey. "I'll see you at home."

"Mr. Chamberlain, wait! Each pile of dirt you dump in there is destroying the environment and putting the Monarch butterfly at risk, not to mention all the birds and other wildlife." Like my *mom*, I wanted to say, but I fought back the urge.

"Green means green!"

"Butterflies not Boutiques!"

"Whoa, whoa, whoa! Nobody is *destroying* the environment." Mr. Chamberlain held up his hands and raised his voice so the crowd could hear. "Chamberlain Construction is a *green* company. Why do you think we've committed to this urban garden idea?"

"So," I continued over the sound of the revving propellers,

checking the information on Luke's phone to make sure I got it right, "are you telling us that you've had a full Environmental Assessment? Because it doesn't seem too *green* to fill in a marsh full of a species of interest."

Mr. Chamberlain turned to me and reddened. He looked back to one of his pinheads and whispered something in his ear. Pinhead shuffled through his briefcase nervously and produced a paper after a few minutes of frenzied searching. Lainey's dad scanned the document quickly and produced it for us to see.

"One of these, you mean?"

I took the paper in my hand.

It was, indeed, an Environmental Assessment. My heart sank. Of course Mr. Chamberlain had jumped through all the hoops. The guy owned a multimillion-dollar construction company.

Pinhead snatched the document back from me and stuffed it in his briefcase.

"So see? Chamberlain Construction is *committed* to the environment. We're even putting in a Rainforest Café in the new wing. You kids are going to love it." Mr. Chamberlain winked at me like I was a first grader and disappeared into his helicopter with his pinhead posse. But just as they were getting in, the turbulence from the propellers made a few papers flutter out of the pinhead's briefcase.

Lainey stooped to pick them up and waved them toward the helicopter, but it had already lifted off and swept over the crowd on its way back to the golf course.

Everyone must have decided it was no use to continue our rally, because I felt the pats on my back as protesters dumped their signs and butterfly wings into Chelse's supply box.

"Hey, wait!" Cori called out over them. "This isn't over. They can't just do this."

But people were already heading for their cars and the campers were being herded back onto the Camp Whycocomagh bus.

"No. We don't have a case." My eyes blurred with tears, thinking the whole rally had been for nothing. "They have every right to be building where they're building."

"And here's the proof," Lainey said as she stalked over toward us, waving what looked like the Environmental Assessment in the air. She stuffed the papers in my hand. "Are you happy now?"

"I'm sorry, Lainey." I reached out to touch Lainey's arm, but she turned and walked away.

Luke, Trey, Cori, Chelse, and Bridget all huddled around me as the crowd dwindled, offering encouraging words.

"Thanks, guys." But as the construction trucks rumbled to a start and headed down to the site once more, my stomach twisted in a horrible gut-wrenching knot. If the epically powerful web presence of Chelse Becker couldn't help save Mom, what chance did I have?

Chapter Fifteen

I SAT ON A LARGE rock by the ocean, just down the hill from the construction site, waiting for Dad to pick me up. The crowd was long gone, the trucks had restarted their caravan back and forth through the chain-link gate, and the gang was catching a ride back to Main Street in Bridget's van. I suppose I could have gone with them, but the thing I wanted most was to be alone.

Large waves crashed against the rocks where I sat. On one hand, I wished the surf would grab hold and sweep me out to sea. On the other, I wanted to run far, far inland and never see the ocean again.

I imagined the sentries blocking the mouth of the culvert underwater and the locked chain-link gate behind me. I'd failed Mom on both land and sea. Even after everything that had happened, nothing had changed.

Someone sat down beside me.

"Luke." I wiped my eyes with the sleeve of my T-shirt and sniffed louder than I had planned.

Luke leaned over, nudging my shoulder with his. "Hey."

"I thought you guys were all gone. Didn't you go with Trey and Cori?" I turned to see if the others were with him.

"I was going to, but then I remembered you still have my phone." He smiled his adorable curvy-lipped smile.

"Oh." I felt in my pocket and realized I'd gone totally klepto on him. Reese would have been proud. I stood on the rock, pulled out his phone, and handed it to him. "Sorry."

"No." Luke slipped his phone into the side pocket of his board shorts. "I'm the one who's sorry. I should never have gotten your hopes up about that Environmental Assessment thing."

"You were only trying to help." I waved a hand back in the general direction of the mall parking lot. "In fact, everyone's been so amazing—even if they don't understand how this is about more than just butterflies for me. Much more."

"For me too," Luke said quietly. That's when I realized this was bigger than just me and Mom. The tidal pool was important to all mers, Luke included.

"I just don't know what to do next." I jumped from rock to rock, trying not to slip into the crashing surf. Luke followed behind, step for step. He picked up large rocks along the way and tossed them into the water beside me, splashing my jean shorts. "Hey, are you trying to soak me?"

"Maybe." Luke laughed. "Or if I'm lucky I'll knock out one of those culvert guys."

That's when something occurred to me.

"Where is that thing anyway?" I followed the shoreline, trying to figure out where the large metal culvert could be, but the water came all the way up to the rocks making it impossible to find. I scrambled up the bank to the road.

"What are you looking for?" Luke asked.

"That spot where the road bumped up a little." I scanned the road. "There!" I pointed.

We followed the hump back to the water. The culvert was still underwater but even deeper than the last time we'd checked. I listened and could just make out the faint ring of the sentries over the pounding surf. Luke must have heard it too.

"So, I should aim for down there, huh?" He picked up another rock and heaved it into the water, but we both knew it would take more than a slowly sinking rock to get past those guys. But seeing Luke tossing rocks into the water reminded me of something.

"You remember that puddle on the beach below Toulouse Point, where we first heard Reese?" I asked.

"You mean the one with the crabs and barnacles that got trapped at low tide?" Luke asked.

"Yeah. I'm just wondering, do tidal pools work the same way?"

"Maybe. I'm not really sure," Luke responded.

I looked down into the water, thinking through my idea and hoping I was right. If the barnacles and crabs got trapped in that puddle when the tide went out, would the same thing happen to the tidal pool? Did the tide go down far enough so that we could actually walk through the culvert?

"When is low tide?" I asked excitedly.

Luke had his cell phone out. His fingers flew over the screen for a few minutes. "According to Weather.com it'll be low tide at 7:32 p.m."

I looked at the time on his cell phone. It was 1:23.

"Darn. That's still six hours away. How low does the tide get here?"

"It's about a five foot drop at my grandfather's place." Luke looked down into the water. "That looks deeper than five feet."

"Yeah, but if it's shallow enough, the sentries might not be able to swim through," I said.

"Only problem is it'll still be light out at 7:30." Luke rubbed his chin and looked down into the water.

"We have to try, though, don't we? When it's dark?" I looked back at him.

"I'm in." Luke slipped his phone back into his pocket and hopped onto a higher rock to get a better look.

"Yeah. Except I'd rather not drag everyone else into this. All those people up there. Plus Chelse. And Cori and Trey. Bridget." I glanced back at the mall parking lot feeling sad that they'd all put so much effort into the rally only to have it all fall apart. "If this is another dead end, I'd rather not have an audience. So...just us?"

Luke held out his hand.

"Just us." He took my hand to help me up to the rock

where he stood. My heart quickened as I stepped onto his rock and realized how close we were standing once I made the trip over. My face was inches from his, close enough to see a new spray of summer freckles across his cheeks and to smell the coconut sunscreen scent of his skin.

Just kiss him, you idiot, I thought, ignoring Dad's voice droning in the background. A whole flock of butterflies fluttered in my stomach and my face grew hot. But if we kissed again that would make him my boyfriend, probably, and me his girlfriend, I guessed. What then? How lame would it be to have a boyfriend and not actually be allowed to date?

I turned my head to give myself a chance to think, but just then, my phone rang.

"Sorry. Excuse me." I shuffled on our now seemingly teeny tiny rock and struggled to get the phone out of my pocket without accidentally knocking Luke into the ocean. "Dad, where are you? I think I might have a solution to our problem. Just meet me at the shore below the mall, okay?"

"I'll be there as soon as I can. Don't do anything until I get there, okay?"

"Yeah, okay, okay. But hurry," I said hanging up.

Luke looked at me slyly.

"So. Just us plus your dad, then?" He took my hand and helped me up the bank to wait for Dad.

"Sorry." I looked back at the rock where we'd stood and gave myself a mental slap upside the head for ruining a perfectly romantic moment. Did Luke think I didn't like him now? Argh! Why did I have to be such a dating dork?

"Actually, it's perfect." Luke picked a long strand a grass and put it between his lips. "Your dad can drive the get-away car."

By the time it was dark enough to launch Operation Culvert, the tide was low but rising. It had rained since dinnertime, and now a steady cold drizzle fell, adding to the eerie darkness. A knee-deep stream flowed out from the culvert, down the shore, and to the ocean about ten feet away.

"There's no way those mers can get up here." Dad shined the light from his flashlight helmet up and down the shallow stream and held a hockey stick over his shoulder, ready to strike at any time.

"I wonder if they stayed in the ocean or if we'll find them waiting in the tidal pool." I waved my flashlight into the hollow vastness of the dark culvert. The light bounced off the corrugated metal walls.

"Well, either way, there are three of us and only two of them, right? Speaking of which, where's Luke?" Dad spun around and nearly took my head off with his hockey stick.

"Whoa there." I ducked. "Easy with that thing, Gretzky."

"Oh, good. There he is." Dad's helmet light spotted Luke scrambling down the bank to the shore. "Are they gone?"

"The security guard just left for the night," Luke said as he joined us. "We should be good to go."

"Perfect." I'd been waiting all day for this moment. It was a relief to have it finally arrive. "So the plan is we go in, get Mom, and get her into the Merlin 3000 if she hasn't finished transforming, right?"

"Yeah." Dad hesitated. "About that—"

"What?" I wasn't sure how many more surprises I could take.

"Well, the computer had to be rebooted after Eddie and I made some modifications," Dad said.

"Isn't it working?" I cried.

"We just haven't had the time to recalibrate it yet," Dad said quietly.

"Dad!" I cried.

"Sorry. I can go back to the trailer now and see—"

"The tide is rising," Luke reminded us.

"Okay, okay." I closed my eyes and tried to stay calm. "The longer we stand around here the less chance we have of making it through that culvert. Electronic devices." I held out my hand for Dad's and Luke's cell phones and stashed them in the waterproof bag inside my backpack. "Let's go."

I waded into the knee-deep water and crawled on my hands and knees to enter the culvert, followed by Luke and then Dad. I knew I could easily mer-micize if I inhaled water for a few breaths, so I kept my head well above surface.

"How long is this thing, anyway?" Luke asked as we sloshed through the tunnel.

"Not sure." I shined the flashlight in front of me, but it didn't help much. Plus, a knocking sound reverberated against the top of the culvert, making it hard to concentrate.

"Dad!" I turned and caught the beam of his headlamp

straight in the eye, burning pinpricks of light onto my retinas, which didn't help the freaked out feeling running through my body. "Could you tuck your hockey stick under your arm so it doesn't bang against the ceiling? Not exactly stealthy, you know what I mean?"

"Oops, sorry."

The walls of the narrow, four-foot wide metal culvert felt claustrophobic as we crawled through. Wondering if the mer sentries could actually swim in the knee-deep water, my heart rate quickened. Or what if they'd ramped up security and added a night shift at the construction site? Maybe Grumpy McGrumpypants was waiting for us on the other end of the culvert!

I'd managed to whip myself into a big ball of nerves, but finally, after another thirty feet or so, I could see a circle of twilight up ahead.

"I think we're almost there," I whispered over my shoulder and tried to steady my breathing, which was quick and uneven from the slog through the culvert. I couldn't believe we'd actually made it. We were SO close to discovering whether or not Mom was safe!

I crawled out of the culvert and took a step forward, but the water was deeper than I'd expected.

"Ahrkk—" I fell forward with a splash, dropping my flashlight into the water. Someone (or something) grabbed my arm! "Get off me!" I cried as I lashed out, working to find my footing.

"Jade?" Dad called out, but soon I heard another splash,

complete with a wave of water knocking me off my feet once more.

"Dad!" Had someone got him too?

I struggled away from the hand on my arm to try to get to Dad, whacking someone in the head in the process.

"Ow!" It was Luke. "I was only trying to help."

"Oh, sorry!" I brought a hand to my mouth, realizing that the hand on my arm had been his.

"It's okay." Luke laughed. "Just remind me not to meet you in a dark alley. You okay, Mr. Baxter?"

"Yeah, I'm good," Dad replied.

Finally, after a few minutes of stumbling and splashing, we managed to drag ourselves to the edge of the pond.

"You didn't breathe anything in, did you?" Luke asked.

"No, just a mouthful and it's disgusting," I replied. I'd caught a splash of water in the mouth and sputtered out the mucky taste. All those truckloads of earth must have started running off into the water. The rain was only making things worse.

"Let's start looking." Dad's headlamp flickered on and off from his unexpected dunk.

"Where do we begin?" I looked around, trying to make sense of our surroundings. "And how are we going to find our way back to the culvert to get out? I won't be much help. I lost my flashlight when I fell."

"Why don't I stay here?" Luke suggested. "Call out when you're ready to come back and I can flash my flashlight to lead the way."

"Are you sure?" I asked. "Shouldn't we all stick together?"

"Only if we all want to get *arrested* together when we can't find our way back," Luke joked.

"He's got a point," Dad said. "I'd rather not have to get a father-daughter jail cell."

I laughed and turned to Luke before setting off.

"Yell if you see something, okay?"

"You got it."

Mom? I rang out over the water for what seemed like the millionth time.

We'd traveled around the edge of the tidal pool for over an hour and found nothing. It was slow going in the dark and rain, and the mucky spots along the way made progress slow. Plus, Dad's headlamp kept flickering and only lit five feet ahead of us.

"I think we're about three quarters of the way around," Dad said.

I was wet and cold and beyond frustrated by the time we reached the stand of trees at the far end of the pond. "What if we don't find her? What if something happened?"

Just then, a light flashed from across the water. "Is that Luke?" My heart skipped a beat. "Maybe he saw something. Luke!"

"Ja—" I heard his yell across the water about a hundred feet away. The light from his flashlight waved in random zigzags for a few seconds accompanied by another yell and splashing. Then the light went out.

"Oh no! *Luke!*" I grabbed Dad's arm. A big red panic button in my head set me off in a fit of guppyish, gulping cries. "What's happening to him?"

"I'm coming, buddy!" Dad called out to Luke. He slapped his flashlight helmet on my head. "Wait here."

"But you won't be able to see!" I said between fits of panic. "How are you going to find him?"

"Just stay put and whatever you do, *don't* go in the water or you're grounded until you're sixteen." Dad crashed through the trees like a bear on a blueberry mission.

"Be careful!" I wiped the streaking tears from my eyes, worrying it would be the last time I'd see him, Mom, *or* Luke. The last thing I spotted in the flickering lamplight was Dad's hockey stick slashing branches as he disappeared into the trees.

Now Mom was still nowhere to be found, something was up with Luke, and Dad had left me standing alone on the banks of a dark, creepy looking pond. I couldn't help thinking that my current situation had all the makings of a really scary slasher movie.

I hadn't been that scared since Finalin and Medora trapped me and Mom in the creek back in Talisman Lake. But this felt far worse. What if Mom hadn't survived this time? What if Luke was in danger too?

I took a few long, deep breaths to keep from completely freaking out and glanced across the water, trying to find the spot where I'd last seen Luke's flashlight, but I couldn't see anything. A few minutes later, I heard Dad's voice echo through the culvert.

"Luke!" Dad called.

"Dad!" I yelled out, desperate for him to answer. Why was he yelling for Luke? Wasn't he where we left him?

"Dad!" I called again.

All I could make out from his answer was a hollow sounding "gonna go see…" and "stay there."

"Wait! I'll go with you!" I called out but he didn't answer. "Dad!"

But it was no use; he was gone. I was really crying by then, blurring everything around me. And just to make things worse, the clouds moved over the moon and my headlamp kept flickering.

Mom? I tried ringing out her name one more time out of desperation.

I heard the crack of a branch behind me and spun around.

"Who's there?" I yelled. I saw a flash of luminescent eyes in the light of my headlamp. Then the eyes turned into the profile of a raccoon that scampered off through the bulrushes. I scanned the pond again and took a few deep breaths to try and get my heart rate back to normal.

Ma…wmm.

A noise took me by surprise. I turned back to the place where the raccoon had popped out. I saw a leg by a nearby tree. Then an arm. Then the bright paleness of a face shone in the lamplight.

I blinked, not understanding what I was seeing at first. Could this be real? Could it really be her?

Then I saw her. All of her. I opened my mouth to speak, but my voice came out as a whisper.

"Serena?"

Chapter Sixteen

S ERENA SLID BACK BEHIND the tree. I slipped off my backpack and took out a blanket from the water-proof bag.

"Serena, it's me, Jade." I held out the blanket and walked toward her carefully, trying not to spook her. "You remember?"

I hadn't seen Serena since her parents, Finalin and Medora, had blackmailed me into freeing her from Talisman Lake along with Mom a few weeks before. She was taller than I'd imagined and younger—about my age. A horrible thought occurred to me. Was it Serena's arm I'd seen in the tidal pool with Cori? Had I risked everything to free her instead of Mom?

Serena looked past the tree trunk and held her hand up against the light of my headlamp. I twisted my helmet to the side so the light didn't flash right into her face.

Sorry, I tried to find my mermaid voice. Even though I was probably saying it all wrong, since my Mermish was still definitely rusty, it seemed to have an effect because Serena took a small step toward me. *Here, take this blanket.*

I wrapped the blanket around Serena's shivering shoulders. She grasped the fabric and hugged it around herself.

How— I started to ask, but as I spoke, Serena took my hand and led me through the trees, stiff-legged like a newborn fawn. At first, I thought she was leading me to the culvert, but we headed into the dark stand of trees. After a few minutes, we stopped by a fallen tree trunk

No, come with me. I pulled on her hand, trying to direct her toward the culvert. We'd have to hurry, otherwise the tide would be too high and we'd be stuck there until morning.

Ma...wmm. Serena crouched down beside the tree trunk.

Only it wasn't a tree trunk. It was a person. With arms and legs and hair, huddled on the ground. Could it be? After all this time and so many dead ends, had I finally found her?

"Ohmigod! Mom?" I lunged toward her and pulled at the branches and leaves covering her body. My head registered a jumble of different thoughts at once. How long had she been there? Was she okay? Was she even alive? "Dad! *Dad!* She's here!"

"Jade?" Mom's voice was barely a whisper.

"Mom!" She *was* alive! I wanted to scream and dance around, but there was no time to waste. Where was Dad? We had to get her to safety.

"I can't believe I finally found you! Dad!" I tried again.

My hands shook as I fumbled in my backpack for another blanket. My words came out in a long babble as I tried to cover her as best I could. "Are you hurt? What have you been eating—are you thirsty? Do you want some water?"

I pulled a water bottle from my backpack and Mom and Serena both drank thirstily.

"Serena changed quicker…been waiting for two…three days?" Mom shivered violently and tried to stand. "Couldn't get out…the fence."

"I know, I know." I put her arm around my neck and helped her stand. Serena did the same. "It's a construction site. There's a way out, but we have to hurry."

We half-carried, half-dragged Mom through the trees toward the general direction of the culvert. I could see glimpses of the chain-link fence a few dozen feet to my right, so I knew if I could just keep that in view, I'd hit water and then the culvert soon enough.

"Ooof!" I tripped and stumbled when my foot sank into a mushy area of grass.

Mom gasped beside me. "Slower?"

"No." I got to my feet. Serena readjusted the blanket over her shoulders and tightened her grip around Mom from the other side. "The water is getting higher. We won't be able to get through the tunnel if we don't hurry."

I'd finally found her. She was alive! She had legs! Nothing was going to keep me from getting her to safety. I swung my head back and forth, trying to shine the headlight's beam to see where we were heading. Finally, the light caught a flash of metal a few yards away.

"Over there." I pointed. The water rose to my waist as

we waded toward the glinting culvert. I grasped Mom and held my free hand out in front of me. Finally, my fingers met the cool metal.

"Through here!" I went first, scrambling through the low culvert backward so I could pull Mom along as I went. The tunnel was two thirds full, thanks to the rising tide, so I kept my chin up, out of the water, and hoped my flashlight helmet didn't fall off. If only I could make it to the other side and back to the beach, Mom could finally come home. Hopefully, Luke and Dad would be on the other end of the culvert and not a couple angry sentries. "Are you guys okay?" I whispered to Mom and Serena, trying to keep our group moving.

"Yes," Mom answered but her voice was labored and hoarse.

I didn't dare call out to see if Dad was on the other side of the culvert. What if the mers heard me? Hopefully, he was making good use of his slap shot over the sentries' heads if they were causing problems.

Something brushed up against my leg.

"Ah!" I called out.

"What is it?" Mom asked.

"Something's down there!"

"Alzear," Mom whispered.

Reese's Uncle Alzear?

"What's he doing?" I kicked my legs through the water to stop him. But all of a sudden, I felt a force pulling me along the tunnel.

"He's helping us," Mom said.

After a few seconds, we emerged from the culvert on the beach side. I scrambled out of the stream, tugging Mom and Serena behind me.

Dad was there, brandishing his hockey stick. "Where is he? Where did that guy go?" He slapped at the water, wild-eyed and crazy-haired.

"Dad!" I called. "Dad! I've got her."

That's when he noticed Mom and dropped his stick. "Michaela?"

"Yes! And she's got legs!" I exclaimed, relieved that we wouldn't have to put the Merlin 3000 to the test, given its technical difficulties.

Mom lifted her head. "Dalrymple?"

I chuckled. Hearing Mom call Dad by his first name never got old. "Dalrymple" just went to show that Gran either had a ridiculous sense of humor or was under the influence of some serious pain medication when he was born.

Dad stumbled toward us, his hand to his mouth. I could see by the dim moonlight that he was soaked, his shirt was untucked, and his glasses sat precariously on his nose.

"Yes, Micci, yes." He took Mom from me and picked her up in his arms. She looked so small and fragile now that I could see her properly. He brushed her hair back from her face and kissed her gently.

"Dal." Mom leaned her head against his chest. Dad's face creased into a sob. He tried to hold back, but soon his whole body sagged in relief.

Serena crawled from the river behind us and stood uncertainly.

"Um, Dad? There's someone else." I turned my headlamp in Serena's direction. She blinked away the glare.

Dad looked up and his face registered confusion.

"Luke?" Dad wiped his eyes in the upper sleeve of his shirt. "No. Who's this?"

"You remember our friends Medora and Finalin back in Talisman Lake?" I asked. Dad still looked confused. "This is their daughter, Serena."

"Oh?" A look of understanding crossed his face. "Oh, I see."

"Wait." I looked around, trying to find Luke. "Where *is* Luke?"

Dad squeezed his eyes shut and blinked. "He wasn't here when I got through the culvert. Maybe he went for help?" Dad looked down into Mom's face, but she was barely conscious. "Let's get your mom back to the car, so she can be comfortable and we can look for him."

"No, wait." Mom lifted her head. She seemed to be trying to listen. I heard the rings too but had trouble understanding. "Alzear says there was a mistake. They thought Luke was a poacher."

"A what?" I asked, my heart in my throat. Whatever it was, it didn't sound good.

"A human mer hunter. The other sentry pulled Luke underwater and he changed. Alzear tried to reason with him, but he's taken Luke to the Council."

I collapsed onto the beach, not believing what I was hearing. Luke was now a mer.

The drive home was quiet. We finally convinced Serena to get in the car, but she spent the whole car ride with her face and hands plastered against the passenger side window like she was on the Behemoth roller coaster at Magic Mountain.

Mom fell asleep almost immediately, wrapped up in one of the dry blankets from the trunk, where we'd also found one of my spring jackets for Serena. My XL windbreaker hung loosely around Serena's narrow shoulders even though she was about two inches taller than I was.

"What's going to happen to Luke?" I asked.

"We'll get the Merlin 3000 to Eddie's house on the coast. Hopefully, he'll show up there." He pulled out his cell to call Eddie.

"But the Merlin 3000 doesn't even work!" I yelled.

"Jade," Dad said quietly, "Eddie will try to get it back online while we wait. I'm sorry but that's the best we can do for now."

I stared out the window as the rain streamed down the glass. What had I done? I'd been so focused on getting to Mom that I'd sacrificed Luke in the process. Life suddenly started to feel like a cruel, warped joke.

Dad had the heat cranked to keep everyone warm, but we smelled like a moldy bog and were full of sand and mud, which didn't help. Despite the rain, I rolled down my window to try and get some fresh air just as we crossed the drawbridge over the canal. Serena leaped across the back seat, crawling over me to see out my window to Talisman Lake.

Maw-rmm!

"What the—?" I asked. "Get off me!"

Dad ended his call. "Whoa there, Serena. Jade, did you show her how to get her seat belt on?"

"You're kidding me, right?" I asked, trying to untangle myself from her arms, the blanket, and her long matted hair.

"She hears them." Mom turned back toward us from the front seat. *Serena, honey, sit back.* Mom placed her hand gently on Serena's shoulder. She jumped back at first, but then turned to Mom and seemed to calm down enough to sit back down on the seat.

Maw-rmm.

Yes, it's her, Mom rang quietly. *But remember what we talked about. Your mother and father wanted you to be free of Talisman Lake. They didn't want you to be imprisoned like they were.*

Serena leaned against her rain-splattered window and cried quietly. I adjusted the extra blanket over her, trying to cover up her shaking legs but secretly wished I'd left her back in Talisman Lake when I'd had the chance. After a few minutes of driving through town, we finally reached our dark, quiet street. Eddie and the Martins were already waiting by our driveway.

Trey came running up to my partially open window as Dad put the car in park. "Why didn't you guys tell us where you were going? We could have helped you!"

I opened the door and slinked out. "I'm sorry. We didn't—"

"Didn't what?" I'd never seen Trey like this. His usual happy-joking self was gone, replaced with a flash of anger behind his eyes.

"I'm sorry, Trey. I..." But what could I say? I'd lost his brother.

"Trey? Help us out here?" Eddie whispered from the open garage as he started hitching the trailer to his truck.

Dad already had Mom partway up the walk. I let out a shaky breath and went over to Serena's side to help her out of the car and into the house.

"Home." Mom was sitting on the sofa in the living room with her eyes closed when I finally got Serena inside.

"Yeah, Mom. You're finally home." I crawled onto couch and hugged her tightly as Serena stood at the door, staring at the hall light.

I thought back to how I'd rescued Mom from Dundee and bargained with Finalin and Medora to get her across the locks. How Reese had led me to the culvert only to be turned away by the sentries. The rally and how hard we'd worked to finally get through the culvert. My whole body shook with relief as I hugged her, now skin and bones from the hell she'd been through over the past year.

But Mom was home, finally home.

I just hoped I hadn't risked too much to get her there.

It was 3:00 a.m. by the time everyone got to bed. I finally convinced Serena to take a bath, then to take another one after her unfortunate accident. It was like having a toddler in the house, showing her how to use the toilet and get ready for bed. Yes, it was all brand new to her, but after arm-wrestling her into a pair of my old pajamas and trying fifteen different sleeping options before she wedged herself under my bed, she was definitely getting on my last nerve.

So when my cell phone rang at half-past stupid o'clock, I swore whoever it was, they were going down. It didn't help that Serena was freaking out like a trapped mackerel underneath my bed.

Eeeeiiii!

"Serena! Shussh." I stumbled out of bed, realizing it could be news about Luke. I was suddenly wide-awake. I dumped the stuff from my backpack onto my bed and sorted through Dad's and Luke's cell phones before finding mine.

"Hello?" I yelled into the phone over Serena's screeching.

"Jade! I tried your cell like six times last night. What happened? Where were you?"

"Cori! You'll never believe what happened." I put a finger in my ear, trying to talk over the screeching. Dad stuck his head in to see if he could help, but I just waved him away with a thumbs-up. He grabbed his cell from my bed and headed downstairs.

"What?" Cori asked.

"It's my mom—"

"Did you find her?" she asked in a hushed, hopeful tone.

"We did!" I answered, tears welling up again, partly from relief and partly from the other bit of news I had to share.

"You must be so happy! I'm so happy—" Her voice choked off the end of her sentence when she heard my sniffles. "But there's more?"

Talk about an understatement.

"Yeah, there's more. Have you talked to Trey since yesterday?" I asked. She didn't answer. "Luke is gone. He was guarding the culvert and the sentries took him."

"Oh no, Jade. I'm so sorry, that's so messed up." She paused for a second while Serena went into another fit of wailing when my alarm clock went off to wake me up for my 9:00 shift at Bridget's. I pressed Snooze and peeked under my bed to reassure her, but she was crouched into a little ball with her back turned.

"Is your alarm clock broken or something?" Cori asked.

"Um, no. That's the third part of this drama-rama." I cradled the phone between my ear and my shoulder and went through my piles of T-shirts and shorts on my dresser, trying to figure out how I was going to find something for Serena to wear given that she was about half my pants size.

"What do you mean?" Cori asked.

"You'll see when you get here." I thought for a second, then snuck a peek at Serena under my bed again. "Hey, if you've got any spare Cori Originals hanging around, why don't you bring them over? I've got someone who could use a stylist."

"Oh," Cori said, "sounds interesting. What about shoes?"

I laughed, wondering how hard it would be to get Serena into a pair of summer sandals considering the pajama episode from the night before.

"Sure. And safety goggles if you have them."

Chapter Seventeen

BIGGEST HEAD TRIP IN the history of the universe? Walking downstairs to breakfast and seeing Mom standing at the kitchen counter, sipping coffee like a normal person. A two-legged, ten-toed normal person!

"Mm…I missed you." Mom grasped her mug and closed her eyes as I entered the kitchen.

"I missed you too." I hugged her, afraid of crushing her in two.

"Oh." Mom looked up from her mug. "I meant the coffee."

"Ha ha, very funny. Seriously, though, I can't believe you're actually home." My heart threatened to burst with relief at the sight of her as sunshine streamed through the kitchen window. But I couldn't let myself totally enjoy the fact that Mom was home. Not with Luke still missing. I spun open a bag of bagels and popped one into the toaster oven, wondering what Luke was eating that morning—if he'd eaten anything at all. "Any news from Luke?"

"Not yet. Your dad's at Eddie's. They've been out patrolling with the boat since dawn. How's Serena?" Mom took another sip of her coffee and sat gingerly at the kitchen table. It would be a while before she was back to her old self, judging by her slow movements. The last year had been tough on her.

"I taught her how to use a toothbrush and now she's trapped in front of the bathroom mirror, thinking there's another mer-girl in there. She's been talking to herself for the past thirty minutes."

I sat at the table next to her.

"Thanks for taking care of her last night. I just..." Mom reached out and stroked my ponytail. I'd forgotten she used to do that. "I couldn't leave her all by herself in the ocean. Not after the promise I made to Finalin and Medora."

I leaned my head against her shoulder.

"I get it," I said quietly, but I couldn't help but feel cheated, knowing that from now on I'd have to share Mom with Serena. Plus, could she even *be* my mom when everyone thought she was dead? "How are we going to do this anyway? It's not like you can walk around town acting like you didn't drown last year."

"Well, for starters, " she said picking up a copy of one of my *Teen Cosmo* magazines from the table. The page was turned to a hair-color ad. "I was thinking of going blond."

"People dye their hair all the time. Are you sure that's going to be enough to fool everyone?"

"I'll cut it too and maybe get some colored contacts. Oh, and I'm now your Tanti Natasha from an obscure South Pacific Island," Mom added, taking a bite of toast and jam. "Tonganesia or something."

"My aunt? Ouch." I burned my hand on the toasted bagel and blew on my fingers. "What about Serena?"

Speak of the devil, Serena walked into the kitchen in my Cinderella pajamas carrying a toothbrush like it was the Olympic torch.

"You mean your Tonganesian cousin Serena?" Mom asked. "She's still learning English so it'll be perfect."

Perfect. I'd just lost my mom and gained an aunt and a cousin from the old country.

Just perfect.

"I think the blue pantaloons look best with the chartreuse chemise." Cori adjusted the fabric belt around Serena's teeny waist.

"Why does she stand still for you?" I mumbled through a mouthful of toothpaste as I leaned against my bedroom's doorframe. Cori's offbeat Cori Original designs were a perfect disguise for a mer-girl masquerading as a cousin visiting from an unknown, remote South Pacific island. "She almost took my head off when I tried to get the pajama top over her head last night."

Cori gave me a scornful look.

"Well, the Cinderella pajamas were your first mistake. Honestly, Jade, have I taught you *nothing*?" Cori arranged

Serena's super long hair around her face. "This is a girl who obviously appreciates fashion."

Pretty. Serena ran a hand along the silky top and smiled broadly.

"Great. She's only been wearing clothes for an hour and she's already got more fashion sense than I do." I walked back to the bathroom to spit and rinse, then returned to my bedroom to finish getting ready for my ice cream parlor shift. Mom wanted me to take Serena with me so she could get used to her new life as soon as possible. I was working my shift with Cori, so at least she could help me chaperone.

"Okay, she's ready to hit the town." Cori stood back from her fashion handiwork and beamed. Serena looked amazing, I had to admit. Mom had helped her wash and brush her super-long hair, and it fell in golden brown waves around her face. Cori had even gotten her into a pair of sandals.

"Not so fast." I switched to my mermaid voice and took Serena gently by the shoulders.

If you come with us, you need to try to make a few sounds with your mouth, okay?

Serena nodded tentatively.

"Yesss," I said slowly, showing her how to move her mouth.

"Yer…shhh." She jumped in surprise at the sound from her mouth then smiled, looking to me for approval.

Good. Now if any boy *humans try to talk to you, you just say* "Nnnooo."

"Nnrroo!"

"Close enough." I turned to Cori. "Now we're good to go."

The house phone rang. The one in my room was buried under a pile of clothes, so I ran into Dad's (and Mom's!) room to answer it.

"Hello?" But Mom had already picked up on the phone downstairs.

"It's okay, Jade, I've got it. It's your dad."

"Is he there? Did Luke turn up?!" I screamed into the phone.

"Sorry, honey. Eddie is out looking for him with the boat right now," Dad answered.

My heart dropped to my stomach. I'd messed things up even more than usual. Luke was in trouble and it was all my fault.

"Did you at least get the Merlin 3000 working?" I asked hopefully.

"The motherboard on the laptop blew, so I'll need to get a new one to reprogram it."

"That doesn't sound good," I mumbled.

"It's not ideal," Dad replied. "Listen, I have to make an appearance at work or else my whole research experiment is going to fall apart. I'll swing by the computer store on the way home and we'll talk later, okay?"

I hung up just as Cori entered the bedroom with Serena at her side.

"Everything okay?" Cori asked. I shook my head.

Luke was still missing and the Merlin 3000 was toast. Things were definitely *not* okay.

"Not by a long shot."

Tuesday morning at Bridget's Diner was thankfully quiet, so Serena stayed occupied spinning on the barstools and lining up sugar packets without the inconvenience of too many gawking eyes.

With lunchtime creeping up, though, I was afraid of what to expect.

"Just try it." I turned to see Cori offering Serena a quarter of the BLT I'd ordered for her, but Serena turned her head.

"Good luck with that." I came over from the ice cream cooler. "I've been trying to get her to eat all morning."

I leaned over the counter to talk to Serena in a language she could understand. *You have to eat something. Aren't you hungry?*

Bridget came through from the kitchen with a Big Breakfast order. She set it down on the counter for a second to get napkins and looked from Serena's untouched food to me.

"Something wrong with the sandwich, honey?"

"Oh." I searched for an explanation for Serena's picky eating habits. "My cousin isn't from around here. She's just not used to our kind of food."

"Well, what does she usually eat?" Bridget asked.

"Um. Well, I'm not really sure." I doubted Bridget had seaweed and barnacles on the menu. "Seafood?"

Bridget considered this for a second and then smiled.

"I think I have just the thing." She served up the Big Breakfast to table six, then disappeared into the kitchen again.

The diner's front door bell jingled.

"Trey!" Cori said.

Trey's face was serious and unsmiling. He met Cori at the till.

"I heard about what happened," Cori whispered. "I'm really sorry."

Trey looked around to make sure no one was listening.

"I can't stay. Just came in for something to eat." He took a plastic-wrapped bagel and cheese from the cooler below the counter and placed it next to the cash register. "My dad had to take my mom to the Emergency Room. She had a relapse, probably because of everything that's going on."

"Oh no, Trey. I'm so sorry," Cori said as she rang up the bagel.

"Yeah, is she going to be okay?" I asked.

Trey glanced my way for a half second, then fished in his pocket for money.

"They're trying to get her stabilized at the cottage hospital or else we'll need to take her back to Renworth Hospital in the city." He picked up the bagel and shoved the change into his pocket. "I've got to get back. Grandpa's starting his shift at the lock and someone's got to keep up the patrols."

He pulled the boat keys out of his pocket and waved to Cori.

"See you later." Then he turned and walked out without looking my way.

"He is *so* mad at me," I said quietly.

"Things are just really crazy right now." Cori brushed past me to go back to the ice cream counter just as Bridget emerged from the kitchen with a steaming plate of mussels.

"Our chef, Daniel, is trying a new recipe, so you can tell me what you think." Bridget placed the plate in front of Serena.

Serena touched a mussel and pulled her hand back when she realized they were hot. Then, slowly, she picked one up and slurped the mussel out from between the shell.

"We'll have to work on her table manners," Cori said, looking over her shoulder from the cooler.

"Well?" Bridget asked, smiling.

Serena nodded and grinned.

"Say 'thank you,' Serena," I whispered, touching her hand.

"T-shank shoe," Serena replied, beaming at Bridget.

"You're welcome." Bridget wrung out a steaming cloth from the sink and picked up a dish tub to go clear a booth by the window. "Nothing makes me happier than a satisfied customer."

I stared at Bridget as she cleaned the table where Luke and Trey usually sat, wondering what to do. Mrs. Martin was sick again and Luke's dad was run ragged making sure she was okay. Eddie had his shift at the canal lock during the busiest boating season of the year, and Dad was fixing the Merlin 3000 and trying to avoid a catastrophe at work.

That left Trey wandering up and down the coast of Port Toulouse looking for his brother. How would he even know where to look?

"I need to go find him," I mumbled as I scooped up a Chilly Grizzly Ripple for a waiting customer.

"Huh?" Cori pulled her eyes away from Serena as she plowed through her plate of mussels.

I handed the cone over to the waiting customer and washed my hands in the sink while Cori made change.

"Trey won't find anything from the boat. I need to go find him myself. *Underwater*," I whispered, making sure no one could hear.

"Nuh-uh, nuh-uh, nuh-uh," Cori waved a finger at me. "You keep doing this. You think no one can do anything but you and then you shut us out."

I stared at her, taken aback.

"Don't give me that innocent look," Cori continued. "Why do you think Trey is so mad? You and Luke went off on your little mer-scapade and tried to play heroes, leaving us out of it. Seriously, Jade, how do you think that felt? We're all on the same team here, even if some of us don't have tails."

"Shh," I said, looking around.

Serena looked up for a second as Bridget brought her another plate of mussels. Cori stared at me, tapping her foot.

"What do you want me to say?" I lowered my voice to a whisper. "That I'm sorry? Or that I was only trying to keep you from getting your legs ripped off by a couple homicidal spear wielders."

"Here's what we're going to do," Cori said, all business-like. "You're going to finish your shift and head home with Serena once she stops stuffing her face. Then I'm going to wait for Chelse to come in to work so I can meet you back at the boat with Trey."

I laughed out loud. "Trey is not going to go for any plan involving me."

"Oh yeah?" Cori got an evil look in her eye. "You just wait and see."

"Jade?" Mom called from the living room when Serena and I got home.

I popped my head in to say hi but saw that she'd been sleeping.

"Sorry, I didn't mean to wake you."

"It's okay." Mom pushed her long hair away from her face and took a sip of water from the glass on the side table. She still looked exhausted but very stylish in one of Cori's hand-dyed sundresses. She sat up and smoothed out the fabric. "I hope Cori won't mind?"

"Are you kidding?" I crossed the family room and snuggled with her on the couch. "She'll be happy to know she's on the cutting edge of mer-fashion."

Serena sat at Mom's other side and touched the sundress's fabric. "Prett-ry?"

"Yes, Serena, pretty. So, Mom…" I tried to think of a way to ask her to go to the ocean to rescue my mer-boy crush. It was probably best to stay vague. "Um, Cori and I were thinking of helping Trey with patrols. Would that be okay? I'll even take Serena so you can keep resting."

Mom squeezed my shoulder. "You want to go underwater to find Luke, don't you?"

Yeah. She totally saw right through me.

"I promise I'll be really, really careful."

Mom put the TV's volume on mute and set the remote control on the coffee table. "I don't know. Your dad told me about the last time this happened."

"Yes, but didn't that have a happy ending? You're here, right?" I rested my head on her shoulder.

"But Luke isn't," Mom said quietly.

"I promise I'll just go tell Luke to go to Eddie's," I said. "Otherwise, who knows how long he'll be stuck down there?"

"I feel terrible about everything that's happened." Mom stroked my hair. "I'd go myself but that wouldn't help matters, I guess."

"Exactly! I, on the other hand, can just crawl back out onto the boat once I'm done. It'll all be fine, Mom. I'll be with Cori and Trey and Serena. Please?" I sat up and grasped her hand.

"Hm." Mom considered me with squinting eyes. "You'll stick together?"

"Yes."

"You'll call if anything happens?"

"Yes."

"You'll…"

"Yes, yes, yes!" I assured her.

Mom put her arm around me and kissed the top of my head. "I keep forgetting you're not twelve anymore."

"Does that mean I can go?" My phone buzzed. It was Cori texting me. Trey was heading up the canal with the boat to meet us at the lock. "Like now?"

"Go!" Mom laughed. "I'd offer to drive, but I'm pretty sure my driver's license has expired."

"Thanks, Mom."

I grabbed Serena by the arm.

"Oh, and I also want to start dating!" I yelled as I headed out the door.

Chapter Eighteen

COREESH? SERENA ASKED AS we arrived at the lock. Trey was busy filling the boat's gas tank at the pump by the control tower. He was chatting with his grandfather, Eddie, and basically ignoring me. I checked my watch.

"Cori," I repeated her name, trying to get Serena to say it out loud. "Lunch rush is done so she should be on her way."

"Cor-eesh," Serena repeated.

"That's my name, don't wear it out." A voice came from behind. It was Cori, all right, but with someone else.

"Cori! And Lainey." I blinked three times, wondering why on earth Cori was with Lainey Chamberlain, considering how things had gone at the rally the day before.

"Yes." Cori stepped onto the concrete pier that skirted the canal. "Lainey was at the diner. She says she wants to talk to us."

I was afraid to ask why. Lainey stepped onto the pier and arranged her hair, then faced us.

"Let me start by saying"—Lainey grasped the handles of her shoulder bag—"that yesterday was *the* most embarrassing day of my life."

I cringed and stole a glance at Cori.

"Yeah." I turned back to Lainey. "Sorry about that."

Cori came to my defense. "It wasn't Jade's fault. I was the one who sent you that Facebook invitation, but only because you made fun of Jade's sweatpants."

"Wait." Lainey put up her hand to stop Cori from continuing. She turned to me. "I am sorry about the sweatpants thing, but they really do have cute ones at Sport Mart."

Was Lainey actually apologizing? To me?

"Um, thanks?" I murmured.

"Anyway, I was reading your pamphlet thingy and wanted to talk to you about it." Lainey pulled out the pamphlet from her large shoulder bag. A furry ball of fluff popped its head from the bag and barked.

Aieeiiiaiiiieee! Serena hid behind me and grabbed my arm so tightly I started to lose circulation in my thumbs.

Lainey stared at Serena in surprise. "Who's this?"

"Oh." I hadn't counted on having to tell this story over and over again. I had to keep my story straight. What had I told Bridget? "This is my cousin, Serena. She doesn't speak much English."

"Oh!" Lainey pulled out her dog and set it on the ground. "Well this is Cedric. Come say hi."

Cedric wagged his little tail and yipped a couple hellos.

"It's okay," I said to Serena.

Serena stepped out from behind me and stooped down to take a closer look. Cedric licked her hand. Serena snatched it back in surprise but smiled.

"He likes you," Lainey said.

"He's cute," I said.

"Thanks! Daddy bought him for me yesterday." She scruffed her dog behind the ear and adjusted his faux-leather doggie vest.

"So, why are you here, exactly?" Cori asked.

"Well." Lainey straightened and stuffed the pamphlet back in her bag. "That pamphlet made me really mad at first. I thought you guys were doing all that stuff because you hated me."

"Lainey, it's not like that—" I began.

"I know," she interrupted. "Because then, I actually read the pamphlet and saw some of the stuff people were saying on the Facebook page about the Monarch butterfly and I just wanted to tell you I think it's really cool what you guys were trying to do."

"You do?" I asked, surprised.

"Yes! I mean, there's no reason to shut down a whole construction site over it, but Daddy and I talked about all the things he could do to make the mall project even more environmentally friendly than it already is. He says he needs that paper I gave you first, though."

"The Environmental Assessment, you mean?" I asked.

"Yes, and," Lainey seemed to choose her words before continuing. "Daddy also asked if you could invite your

Butterflies versus Boutiques Facebook people to a beach party at Toulouse Point Park to tell them about his new plans. So"—she looked from Cori to me—"do you think you could do that?"

Cori and I stared at each other, confused.

"I guess," I replied, not exactly sure what I was agreeing to.

"Oh good. Because I've already got forty-seven replies to my Facebook event so far, and I need you guys to invite as many people as you can."

"When is it?" Cori asked.

"Tonight! I wanted to ask Luke to bring his guitar, but he hasn't returned any of my texts. Do you know where he is?"

"No clue," I replied. Which was pretty much the truth.

"Oh, sorry. You guys broke up, right?" Lainey gave me her best pouty-lipped look of sympathy.

I secretly rolled my eyes. It was good to know that Lainey hadn't lost all her evil ways. But 'broke up'? Could you break something up that was never together? All I knew was that I liked Luke. Really liked him. And if anything happened to him, I wasn't sure if I could ever forgive myself for dragging him into this big mess.

"Anyway," Lainey continued, not waiting for my answer, "do you think I could get that Environmental Assessment thing from you? Daddy was really upset when he found out I'd given it to you. He says he really needs it to go ahead with his plans."

"Yeah, sure. I think I have it home somewhere," I said, but meanwhile Cori waved me on board because another boat was waiting for the gas pump and Trey was firing up the engine to get out of the way.

"And you'll invite everyone to the beach party, right? You come too, Serena!" Lainey called out.

"We'll definitely try to make it if we can!" I rushed Serena onto the boat and moved a couple of orange buoys so we could sit next to Cori on the padded bench in the stern.

"But wait a second. Where are you guys going?" Lainey called after us. She stood on the lock's pier, clutching her bag.

"Sorry, Lainey. We really have to go!" I called out.

"That was weird," Cori muttered as I settled onto the seat next to her.

"Yeah," I replied. But it really sounded like Lainey and her dad were trying to make things right, so I felt really bad when the boat shoved off and we left her standing on the dock all by herself.

Lainey fumbled with her shoulder bag and chased us all the way along the canal, screaming.

"Just keep going!" I waved to Trey. I felt terrible for leaving Lainey, but I didn't exactly feel like explaining our little mer scavenger hunt to her. It was already mid-afternoon and there was no telling where Luke was by then.

We traveled down the mile-long canal and left Lainey waving her arms at us at the end of the canal's concrete pier. Soon we were sailing out into Port Toulouse Bay and out into the great blue yonder.

"Watch her for me?" I asked Cori, motioning to Serena, who was huddled like a baby on the bench seat in the stern of the boat. "I need to talk to Trey."

Cori flashed me a peace sign and looked down at her phone. "I'll just do my good deed for the day and post Lainey's beach party invitation on Facebook to make up for ditching her at the canal and everything."

"Cool." I got up to join Trey in the cabin of the boat. He held the boat's steering wheel with one hand and punched a few keys on a computer screen. I took a closer look, seeing it was a fish finder.

"That won't work," I pointed to the screen. "Luke says mers can block the sonar signals on those things."

"True," Trey said without looking up, "but do you think we just tossed Luke into the ocean down in Florida without a backup plan? Cause that would be really stupid, you know."

He was still mad at me. Big time.

"Look, Trey..." But what could I say? This was my fault. I should have never asked Luke to help me, considering he was a mer and everything. "I'm really sorry. I never wanted anything to happen to Luke, trust me."

Trey's mouth twitched. "It's not just that. Well, it used to be just me and him and...never mind."

That's when I got it. The trip to Florida, their whole life, it had been Trey and Luke, two brothers with a secret to keep. Now, here I was, swooping in and shutting Trey out. I gave him a friendly punch in the arm. "Would it help if I promise to never go on any more death-defying mer adventures without you?"

Trey looked up and tried his best not to smile.

"Aw, come on!" I pinched my cheeks and flashed him a goofy grin. "How can you stay mad at this face?"

"No fair." He laughed and grabbed me around the neck and noogied me like a fourth grader.

"Get off me, you moron." I laughed, shoving him away. I pushed the hair away from my face and tried to get a better look at the computer screen. "Okay. So are you going to show me how this thing works or is it a Martin Family trade secret?"

Trey punched a few more keys and turned the screen my way. "Bobby was great with Luke back in Florida, but just in case something went wrong, my grandpa programmed this fish finder to track him underwater."

"It can do that?" I asked, trying to make sense of all the blips and colors on the screen.

"It can now. Mers do have natural sonar-blocking skills like noise-canceling headphones, but my grandpa put a tracker in Luke's watch."

"The watch he wouldn't give up if his life depended on it?" I remembered how he'd held onto it for dear life when I had given my watch to Reese as a peace offering.

"His life kind of *does* depend on it. We didn't tell Luke about the tracker because he was big on doing this whole mer thing on his own, but Grandpa told him the watch was super-expensive and if he ever lost it he'd fillet him like an Atlantic salmon. It's kind of the same technology as the black box they have on airplanes but a little more low-tech, so we need to be pretty close to be able to track it."

"Like, how close?" I asked.

"At least a mile. The closer the better. I got a faint signal this morning, about three miles offshore, but I had to turn back to get gas. That's where we're heading now."

"Oh, awesome!" I glanced out the side window to see where we were going, but it all seemed like a big blue blur.

"Hey, guys?" Cori said from the door of the cabin.

We both turned.

"I think I know why Lainey was freaking out so much back at the canal." She pulled Serena into the cabin behind her. A fluffy ball of fur peeked out its nose from the folds of Serena's flowing chemise.

"Serena!" I sighed, wondering how far Lainey would go to save Cedric from an accidental dognapping.

Cedric perked up and licked Serena's face. Cori rolled her eyes.

"This will not end well."

After an hour or so of sailing, we finally got a faint signal on the sounder.

"See that?" Trey pointed to the screen. The screen flashed "FLUKE1019" whenever it detected his signal.

"Like his cell phone," I murmured, remembering that I'd left his cell phone on my bed.

"That's the same signal I saw earlier, but he could be anywhere within a mile from here. How do we get him to come to us?" Trey asked.

Serena looked up from scruffing Cedric's neck. Her eyes widened in alarm. I heard the ringing too.

"I hear him!" I cried.

"What?" Cori asked.

"Cut the engine for a second?" I motioned for Trey to put the boat in neutral, then strained to hear the faint ring coming from underwater. "Serena, you can hear it too, right?" I nodded toward her, hoping she'd understand.

"Yer-shh."

Cori, Serena, and I rushed out to the main deck of the boat and scanned the water just as the CB radio signal went off.

"*Lady Sea Dragon* from Lock Control, come in!"

Trey answered the call. "This is *The Lady Sea Dragon*, go ahead, Grandpa."

"Hey there, Trey. I just picked up a signal on the First Response Channel. Seems they got an urgent call from a Miss Chamberlain about a diabetic passenger named Cedric on board? Apparently he needs his insulin medicine. Just wanted to give you heads up that the Coast Guard is on its way."

"Rawrff!"

Cedric perked up from Serena's arm, right on cue. She

let him down onto the deck floor where he ran around chasing his tail, then plopped down on the deck, ears twitching.

"A diabetic dog? Leave it to Lainey." Cori shook her head.

"Thanks, Grandpa! We may be coming close to something out here, but we'll keep you posted." Trey hung up the CB radio and turned to us. "Now what do we do?"

We'd finally found Luke, but now the Coast Guard was hot on our tails. Would we be able to find him again if they hauled us back to the harbor? And how much time would we lose in the meantime?

"How fast can this boat go?" I asked, in case we needed to make a quick getaway.

"We use it for water-skiing, so pretty fast," Trey answered. "But the Coast Guard boats are just as fast, if not faster."

I looked out into the water, panicked. Luke was down there somewhere.

"Call my mom and let her know what's going on," I instructed Cori.

"What are you going to do?" she asked as she pulled out her phone.

"If Luke can't come to us, I'm going to go to him." I started unbuttoning my jean shorts and rushed out to the main deck.

"You what?" Trey called after me, hopefully with his hands over his eyes.

"Eyes on the road, captain boy!" Cori yelled.

"Not looking! I promise," Trey called out.

"So you're really going to do this?" Cori asked. "I'm actually going to see you turn into a mermaid? Cool!"

I hopped around, trying to untangle my flip-flops from my jean shorts. "Well, it's not exactly pretty, so don't get your hopes up."

"Go get him, fish-girl!" Cori beamed as she scratched Cedric behind his diabetic ear. I gave her a quick salute and dove into the ocean before I could change my mind.

What I wasn't counting on, though, was the other splash that followed closely behind.

Chapter Nineteen

THE NEXT FEW SECONDS were a flurry of exploding tails, shredded clothing, and water burning through to my lungs. By the time the water cleared, I was so mad, steam probably whistled from my ears.

Are you kidding me? I rang through the water. I spotted Serena looking around, trying to get her bearings.

Help you? Serena's hair swirled around her face as she turned my way.

Argh! You are NOT helping! Now I had to figure out how to get *two* mers back to dry land. But the look on Serena's face was so ready, so willing, so…eager. Was this like what Cori had said? Did I even know how to ask for help?

Okay. Come on, then. I swam over to grab her hand. *But try not to steal anything.*

I saw another mer swimming a couple dozen feet away.

Luke?

But it wasn't Luke. It was Reese. He swam toward us with the speed of a killer whale.

Where's Luke? I rang.

Reese held up his hand. He had Luke's watch on his wrist. *He gave me this. He told me you would come.*

Trey was wrong. Luke had known about the watch the whole time. *But why did he have to give the watch to you?*

They have him. Come!

Just a sec. I popped my head out of the water and called out for Cori. "It's not Luke, but we're going to find him."

"Be careful!" Cori called out as I dove back into the water and followed Reese and Serena to the bottom of the ocean.

Finally, we came to rest behind a curtain of kelp overhanging a rock outcropping on the outskirts of a deserted-looking mer village of low-lying caves.

Where do they have him? Here? I asked, willing my heart to settle in my chest. *Where is everybody?*

Hiding. Reese pointed upward in the general direction of *The Lady Sea Dragon.*

Hiding from the boat? Like a fire alarm? I wondered.

Reese nodded. Did they know boats couldn't detect them? Could they even understand what sonar was and that they had these awesome sonar-blocking skills the Navy would kill for? Probably not.

I'm so happy you're okay. I thought of the last time I'd seen Reese. *I was so afraid of what they would do when they took you and Renata away.*

They let me go but Renata lost her privilege to bring the food, Reese said.

I'm really sorry to hear that, I replied.

Reese nodded, then looked past my shoulder to Serena. His face broke into a broad grin. *And you are back.*

I looked from Reese to Serena. If sparks could fly through water, I was sure I'd be staring at jet streams of steam.

Uh, can we get back to the subject at hand? I asked. *Where is Luke?*

Reese tore his eyes away long enough to focus on our conversation. He tightened his grip on his satchel. *Follow me.*

I followed Reese and Serena through the back alleys of the village. The ever-present danger of *The Lady Sea Dragon* looming high overhead must have really freaked everyone out, because the place was a ghost town.

Reese motioned to an entry in the rock face. *In here.*

A current of water swept against us, like we were going in through the out door. Once inside, Reese led us through a dark, narrow tunnel. It took a few minutes for my eyes to adjust.

What is this place? I asked.

Tribunal. Reese held up his hand for us to stop.

Tribunal? Like a courtroom? Were they keeping Luke under lock and key? I pushed past Reese and grabbed at the dark, slippery walls to propel myself forward. *Where is he?*

Careful. Reese grabbed the back of my shirt and held me back. Just then, three mers crisscrossed our path, along a distant tunnel.

Once they'd gone, we swam until we entered a cavernous space as big as Bridget's Diner but deep and hollowed out, so it looked like a small auditorium. Reese's Uncle Alzear

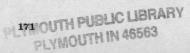

guarded the door. He shook his head slightly at Reese but waved his hand for Serena and me to swim through.

I can't go any farther, Reese whispered.

I get it. But thank you, you've already done so much. I squeezed his hand. Serena gave him a kiss on the cheek.

Uncle Alzear motioned for Reese to go, then blocked us from view so we could hide behind a rock on the upper level of the room. The grotto's walls sparkled with photo-luminescence, like I'd seen once on a *Planet Earth* video, lighting the space with a dim glow.

I pulled back some of the swaying moss from the craggy rock formation to get a better look. The room dipped down into a central meeting area. There, a group of about a dozen adult mers lounged around stone tables filled with seafood. Several mers ate while others talked in groups of twos and threes. Just then, a mermaid with sharp features and graying hair floated into the grotto from a passageway on the far side. The chatting stopped and mers put down their food.

Is the vessel still present overhead? The mermaid raised her eyes upward, even though the grotto's ceiling hid the patrolling boat.

Yes, Dame Council. A younger merman minion with a peach fuzz beard nodded.

Then we must hurry. Attention, everyone. Dame Council floated over the group and paused to consider each of the mers' faces. *You've been gathered here to make a final decision on the boy. Do you swear to make this decision in accordance with our laws?*

Yes, Dame Council, the crowd answered in unison.

Dame Council motioned to her minion. *Bring him in.*

A few minutes later, Peach Fuzz returned, holding Luke by the arm. The sight of him with a tail made my heart leap to my throat and filled me with guilt. He was a mer because of me. Had they hurt him? Threatened him?

I couldn't stand wondering what he'd been through since they had pulled him underwater. Luke had sacrificed so much to help me find Mom. This was my chance to return the favor. I braced my hands against the rock in front of me, ready to kick some mer butt, but Serena put her hand over mine and shook her head, putting a finger to her lips.

Luke's eyes darted from right to left, no doubt searching for a way out, but with Peach Fuzz's hand gripped on his arm and a roomful of mers, things weren't looking good. I wished I could call out to him, to tell him we were there, but what good would that do? We were just three kids against a whole Mermish Council. It was like the Butterflies vs. Boutiques rally all over again.

As Mermish Council, we are charged with the respon-sibility of Absolute Power Over the Sanctity of Mership, Dame Council said, looking down her straight, narrow nose. *I trust you will not make this decision lightly. What say you, Framulus?*

A merman with balding hair and sagging jowls swam over the group and turned to address them. *The boy cannot be left to come and go as he pleases. He risks revealing the Webbed Ones secret to the village. Escort him back to the tidal pool.*

The tidal pool is too dirty, Uncle Alzear said. *It will take many tides to clear.*

What of his family to the north? Another elderly mermaid adorned with many seashell necklaces asked. *No one will discover his secret if we shuttle him there.*

His family? Had the Mermish Council figured out where Luke came from? Could he be reunited with his birth family? Luke's shoulders tensed. Was it fear? Anticipation? Was this what he wanted?

Dame Council consulted with Peach Fuzz. *How long before you can assemble a team?*

We can leave at nightfall, providing the vessel is gone.

Leave? For up north? Take Luke away?

Wait! Luke called out.

A murmur swept over the crowd of mers.

Let the boy speak. Dame Council turned her sharp eyes to Luke.

Luke looked from Uncle Alzear to the other members of Council. He opened his mouth to speak, then stopped. Was he considering it? Did he even have a choice?

They couldn't send Luke north. North, where? It was hard enough finding him today. How would we stand a chance if we didn't even know where to start looking? I had to talk to Luke before that happened, at least to have him understand how I felt—how everyone felt—about him. And about his mom too! Geesh! He didn't even know his mom was back in the hospital.

Come on, boy. Speak up, Dame Council urged. *Though,*

I must warn you...should you decide on this option, you can never return here.

I'll go, Luke said flatly.

No! I shot out from behind the rock without thinking. I could feel Serena's hand skim my tail as I swam out from our hiding place, but she didn't follow.

Well, well. Dame Council examined my YOU CAN'T SPELL AWESOME WITHOUT "ME" T-shirt and glanced back at Luke, who was still wearing a T-shirt of his own. She obviously put two and two together and realized she was dealing with another two-legger because she waved her hand toward me, motioning for the other mers to detain me. *This certainly complicates matters.*

Halt. Uncle Alzear held back several mers from the Council. He grasped my arm lightly. *I've got her.*

Bring her to me, Dame Council bellowed. Uncle Alzear turned and gave me an apologetic look, then pulled me toward the center of the dimly lit grotto.

Luke's eyes widened when he saw me. *How did you get here?* he whispered in English.

I glanced upward for a split second. *By boat with Cori and Trey. Serena is with me,* I whispered back in English, hoping no one caught on to what we were saying.

Serena? he asked. *I thought...*

Enough! Dame Council bellowed. *Once again, this is an open defiance of the Council and our mandate. It will not be tolerated.*

There is only one option for those who defy the Council.

Jowls smoothed his balding head as he spoke. *What of the Freshie prison?*

Mers from all sides turned to consult with one another and several nodded in agreement. The elderly mermaid with the shell necklaces spoke up. *The Freshie prison is only used in extreme circumstances. We have not sentenced anyone there since the last uprising.*

Uprising? Like, against the Council? I stopped to think. Mom had explained that Freshies were criminals, kept in Talisman Lake for their crimes. Was she wrong? Were those people just inconvenient squeaky wheels for the Mermish Council?

These children are no better than the original rebellion leaders, Finalin and Medora, Jowls said.

I looked at Luke. He understood right away. Finalin and Medora were Serena's parents. Sure, they were mean thugs, but had they been shut away in Talisman Lake for some political reason?

Dame Council narrowed her eyes, as if remembering something.

Only then, we were able to justify Finalin and Medora's imprisonment by charging them with the murder of that era's Grand Council. A wry smile crept across her face. *Unfortunate but quite convenient for us, don't you all think?*

A ripple of laughter swept over the Council.

At this, Serena whizzed out from behind the rock, her eyes blazing. *My mother. My father. Framed for a murder they didn't commit?*

Mother? Father? Finalin and Medora have been Freshies well past your age! That can only mean one thing. Jowls looked from me to Luke. *These two are freeing prisoners from the Freshie prison! This cannot stand. It simply cannot stand.*

Mers from all sides talked at once, debating the issue in loud, ear-piercing screeches.

It is time to put this to a vote, Dame Council announced. *All those in favor of imprisoning these three on the grounds of violating the Secrecy Decree and threatening Mermish Sanctity?*

Eleven pairs of hands rose through the water and clapped in some sort of mer voting signal. The elderly woman with the seashell necklaces remained still.

Dame Council eyed her menacingly but continued with her ruling. *Passed.*

I grasped Luke's hand and Serena's too. What would it mean, being shut behind the lock of Port Toulouse canal and becoming a prisoner in Talisman Lake? Finalin and Medora were going to have a conniption fit once they saw me return with their daughter. And what about Luke? Could I get the Merlin 3000 to a place on the lake where he could transform safely? Had Dad even got it working again?

I needed to get to Cori and Trey. Somehow, I needed to get a message back to Mom, Dad, and the others.

Alzear, escort the prisoners to the Freshie prison, the Dame Council instructed.

Uncle Alzear swam to our side and pulled long strands

of thick seaweed from around his torso. He bound our hands together with a sad expression.

The way is clear, Peach Fuzz dude announced after checking outside for the boat.

That could only mean one thing: the Coast Guard had caught up with Cori, Trey, and diabetic Cedric.

The Lady Sea Dragon was gone.

Chapter Twenty

UNCLE ALZEAR WAS THE perfect host for our swim to the Port Toulouse canal even if, technically, he was leading us to our doom.

Traveling was slow, though, because our hands were still bound together like a double three-legged arm race with me in the middle and Luke and Serena at both sides. Plus, I kept whacking my tail against Serena's, sending us all off course.

Sorry, I said for the millionth time.

My apologies—Uncle Alzear looked back to check on us—*but I must keep you bound. If we were to be seen...*

Don't worry, I said. *We'll be a shoo-in for the three-legged race at the next Mermish County Fair.*

I was grateful for the smirk from Luke to help lighten the mood because my jokes were falling flat with Alzear and Serena. Thankfully, the long swim back to the canal gave me an hour or so to talk to Luke and explain everything that had happened with the mall construction and my mom. Who knew what was waiting for us in Talisman

Lake. What if we got separated? What if Finalin and Medora skewered us like fish kabobs?

Wow, a lot can happen in a day. Maybe I should go away more often, huh? Luke joked.

Very funny, but there's something else, I admitted. *Your mom. She's not doing very well.*

Oh…like in the hospital? Luke asked. I nodded. We swam for another few minutes before Luke spoke again. *She's the one who told me it was okay, you know.*

I glanced his way to catch his meaning, but his face was unreadable. *That what was okay?*

She said I could go find my mer-parents once I turned fifteen in October. I guess, being sick, she wanted me to know I had that option.

And back there, when Dame Council asked you if you wanted to go up north to be with them?

Luke laughed. *Well, it was sooner than I'd expected, but it didn't seem like I had much of a choice.*

But if you had a choice—? I began. But just then, Reese swam up from behind and scared the scales off my tail. *Geesh, Reese. We're going to have to put a bell on you.*

You should not be here, Uncle Alzear said quietly, coasting to a stop a few dozen feet from the mouth of the canal leading up to the lock.

Is this what it comes down to? Reese shot a glare his uncle's way. *Imprisoning your own nephew?*

Uncle Alzear's face fell.

It's not up to me. He bowed his head and swam off to talk to the two sentries stationed at the mouth of the canal.

Nephew? I asked. *Alzear's your uncle too?* I looked from Reese to Luke. *And Reese…*

Is my cousin, Luke said with a smile. *We figured it out last night when Reese and Alzear tried to free me.*

And now what does he do? Reese muttered once his uncle was out of earshot. *Lock you up because it's "not up to him"?*

He did what he could, Luke said quietly.

Serena stroked Reese's arm, but meanwhile she shot furtive looks toward the canal as the sound of propellers vibrated through the water. I followed Serena's gaze and could make out two boats tied up along the concrete pier, just inside the canal walls. One I recognized as *The Lady Sea Dragon*; the other one was red and white.

Oh! That's our boat—and the Coast Guard? Luke asked. *What's that all about?*

Rescue mission. Lainey Chamberlain's dog was a stow-away. I could see Lainey standing on the pier snuggling Cedric while a tall woman in a blue uniform seemed to be reprimanding her, probably for failing to mention that Cedric was a dog and not human.

Luke's eyebrows scrunched in confusion. *Do I want to know?*

I shook my head. *No, but I really hope Trey doesn't decide to take the boat to your house on the lake or else that's where we're headed too.*

As if on cue, *The Lady Sea Dragon* shoved off and started to make its way up the canal.

I think I jinxed us, I said.

Uncle Alzear returned and led us partway up the canal. Reese tagged along, despite the murderous glares from the other two sentries posted at the canal's entry.

This is where I leave you. Alzear used the tip of his spear to unbind our hands and hugged each of us. *Be safe.*

Safe? Reese spat.

Alzear turned his back to the other sentries and rang in an almost inaudible tone. *Take heart; there is talk of another uprising. I can't say more, but some of us will stop at nothing to see you free again.*

Serena's eyes widened. As quick as a flying sea monkey, she grabbed Alzear and hugged him tightly. He smiled and scanned the boats making their way up the canal.

Take a few moments, then they must go. Alzear touched Reese's arm before swimming away.

Serena hugged Reese and kissed him on the cheek before she flicked her tail to follow *The Lady Sea Dragon* up the canal. Reese watched her go, his cheeks a deep pink.

Maybe your Uncle Alzear will let you visit on weekends? Luke kidded.

Maybe, Reese said with a smile.

Seriously, though. Luke held out his hand to shake Reese's, then pulled him into a big hug. *Thank you so much for everything you've done for us, man.*

And for helping me find my mother, I added.

Mother? Reese said, his green eyes glinting. *She is safe?*

Yeah, I said quietly. *Is…do you still have your mother?*

Here and here. Reese put his hand to his head then his heart. *But go!*

Keep the watch! Luke called to Reese, then he took my hand and we swam toward the lock.

So, do we have a plan? Luke pulled me through to the lock's holding area as the metal gate on the Atlantic side swung shut, trapping us inside the lock with *The Lady Sea Dragon*.

We still had a few minutes before the other gate opened to the lake side, but I wasn't sure the extra time would help because I didn't have an answer. I'd battled Finalin and Medora before, but the only reason I had won was because I could give them what they wanted: their daughter's freedom. Now I was showing up at their front door, delivering their daughter back to them. Plus, I was bringing a friend. Talk about crashing a party.

Swim like the wind? I offered.

Luke wrinkled his nose. *That was kind of my plan too.*

I looked up through the water to see if I could catch a glimpse of Cori. She stood at the stern of the boat talking to Trey, but I couldn't be sure who else was in the boat. I checked to see how Serena was doing. It couldn't be easy being back here.

Home again. Serena waited under the hull of *The Lady Sea Dragon* as the water level rose to adjust to the lake level. The rush of fresh water into the lock made me want to gag.

Yeah, but don't worry. I'll figure out a way to get your legs back—both of you guys. But I wasn't so sure. Yes, *I* could just crawl out of the water and become human again, but how was I going to get Luke and Serena back on their own two feet?

I slapped the side of *The Lady Sea Dragon*'s hull to get Cori's attention, hoping no one else would notice.

"You made it back," Cori whispered as she hung over the side of the boat. "Is Luke with you? And Serena?" She grabbed a bucket and dunked it into the water pretending she was about to swab the deck or something.

"Yes, and we could really use your help."

"Okay, but make it quick. Lainey's up on the dock talking to the Coast Guard people," she whispered.

I dunked underwater to catch my breath and racked my brain to try to come up with a plan.

"Get the water-skiing tow rope ready off the stern," I said quickly as I resurfaced. "Toss me one of those little orange buoys that were on the bench seat. And get rid of Lainey."

"Gladly," Cori said, handing me a buoy.

I forced the buoy underwater then dove to rejoin Serena and Luke under the hull just as the lock's gate began to creak open to let the Martin's boat sail through to Talisman Lake. A few familiar mers peeked around the big metal barrier, no doubt hoping for a welcoming rush of salty water to pep them up after a long wait in freshwater. I swam out into the lake with Luke as nonchalantly as possible, fighting against the pressure of the buoy against my stomach as it forced itself upward.

Hi, guys! I waved with my free hand, trying to look friendly.

I'm not exactly sure that my gesture was received in the spirit it was intended, because all of a sudden, the underwater realm was filled with ear-piercing screams.

Aieeaieee!

Serena's face lit up. *Mother! Father!*

Medora zipped past all the other mers and screeched cries of relief as Serena emerged from the lock. She swam to embrace her daughter. Finalin, on the other hand, was less than enthusiastic.

You! He pointed and shot me a menacing look. He was still as ugly and scary as last time, except now—thanks to a few Mermish lessons—I could understand what he was saying. Thankfully, Serena and Medora had him in a family hug, buying Luke and me some time to duck, dodge, and dash around the school of mers.

Just keep swimming, just keep swimming, just keep swimming, swimming, swimming, I chanted under my breath to Luke while everyone enjoyed their little reunion. Just because it turned out that Finalin and Medora weren't murderers didn't mean they weren't capable of seriously maiming us.

Gladly, Luke whispered back. *That dude looks like a mob boss.*

Pretty close.

I shot a glance into the lake to see if I could spot *The*

Lady Sea Dragon. The boat had almost reached a point about two hundred feet away, but it looked like it was slowing down. Cori stood at the stern, scanning the water.

I kept the buoy tucked under my stomach, waiting for the perfect time to signal Cori, but it kept pushing me upward, making it hard to swim. We'd only made it about a hundred feet past the lock before the metal gate swung shut. Like it or not, we were stuck in the lake, but if we could just put enough distance between us and the pod of mers...

Glurp!

Our luck ran out when the bright orange buoy slipped out of my grasp and shot up through the water. It popped out from the water's surface, landing back with a splash.

Get her! And him! Finalin motioned for his henchmen, the same ones who were at his beck and call back when I'd been in the lake with Mom. They snapped to attention and began to swim our way.

Swim for the boat, Luke called out, grabbing my arm. By that time, Cori had seen my buoy signal and was shouting for Trey. He steered the boat around and headed in our direction while she tossed the water-skiing tow bar into the water.

But something held me back. *Serena!*

Serena glanced our way, then looked from her mother to her father. Quicker than mermishly possible, she swam to the henchmen, grabbed their weapons, and tossed them aside, then whizzed toward us.

Go, go, go! Luke and I kept swimming for the boat as Serena raced to catch up.

I was the first to grab the towrope and held it out for Luke as he approached. Serena was still a dozen feet or so away, but I had to get the boat heading out into the lake and away from Finalin and Medora. I popped my head out just long enough to yell to Cori, hoping no one would see.

"Get us to my Gran's in Dundee." The Martin's house was too close to town. Gran's would be remote enough for us to do what we had to do—if we could get there.

Trey got the boat turned around, nearly ripping off my arm in the process. Serena had almost caught up, but so had the two henchmen, closely followed by Finalin and Medora. Medora had just gotten her daughter back. It didn't look like she was giving up without a fight.

But neither was I.

Come on, Serena, I called. *You can do it!*

It would have been so easy to leave her there with her family, to get Luke and me to safety. But despite her dog-napping tendencies, Serena was kind of growing on me. Finally, she reached out and grabbed the bar of the towrope.

Hold on tight!

Cori was watching through the water, and I saw her signal to Trey to put the pedal to the metal. All of our necks snapped back with the sheer speed of the boat.

We flipped over to our backs so the rush of water from the propellers wouldn't suffocate us, but I wished I hadn't looked back, because Finalin, Medora, and the mer-goons were gaining on us. I could barely speak against the force of current from the moving boat.

Bf-faster-fff! I rang.

Our high-speed chase continued past the point and well into Talisman Lake. The farther away from the locks we traveled, the fresher and thinner the water felt, and the harder it was to breathe. Thankfully, that meant the mergoons had fallen away, but Finalin and Medora were still in hot pursuit thanks to years of getting used to the freshwater. Serena looked like she was making out okay too, but Luke's mouth was opening and shutting like that goldfish I'd won at the Port Toulouse Fair when I was six.

But Mom had survived being trapped under the Becker's dock in the freshest part of the lake for three weeks. We could do this. We had to!

Bff-just concentr-ff-ate, I rang out to Luke at my side. *Fff-we just need to outrun them-fff.*

Luke turned and smiled at my joke about running, then closed his eyes to zone out and concentrate on his breathing. I wished I could close my eyes, but Finalin was at my tail, hand out to grasp it. Medora was just a few feet behind, calling out to her daughter.

Serena! What is this? What have you done?

But Serena ignored her and reached her tail over to swat her father's hand away when he reached out to grab me. The force of her hit was enough to send him hurtling backward. He righted himself and continued to chase us, but try as he might, our boat was too fast for him to catch up.

Soon, Medora gave up too, and I watched her disappear into the darkness of the water as we sailed farther and farther away.

Chapter Twenty-One

M Y HEART RATE FINALLY settled to a semi-normal rate once we reached a group of islands about half an hour later. Trey had to slow the boat to about half speed because the channels of water between the islands were narrower and shallower than the open lake. My arms ached and my fingers had gone numb around the tow bar, but reaching the islands meant we were almost at Gran's cottage.

By then, Serena had let go of the tow bar and was swimming alongside the boat and keeping up easily, unaffected by the freshwater, probably because she'd lived in the lake her whole life. Luke and I, on the other hand, were panting for breath like we'd just run some of Mr. Higgins's calisthenics drills on Sports Day.

Almost there, I rang to Luke. He looked my way and managed a weak smile, but his eyes were unfocused and his eyelids drooped. *Are you okay?*

Luke nodded but a tremor shook through his body. One of his hands dropped from the tow bar, then the other, and I watched in horror as he drifted away as the boat sailed on.

My face broke the surface of the water. "Stop!"

Cori was at the side of the boat in an instant. She called out for Trey and I heard the engine power down. "What? What is it?" Cori asked, leaning over the stern.

"Luke." I couldn't help it; I took a huge breath of air to keep from suffocating. It burned through to my lungs but gave me the relief I'd been craving since the water changed from salty to fresh. "He let go."

By then, I was breathing air in big hungry gulps. I tried diving back in to go find Luke but resurfaced hacking a mouthful of water. Serena swam around my tail and looked up at me through the water. Her eyes searched mine, trying to figure out what was going on.

Luke! I pointed behind the boat. She understood and took off in his direction.

"He can't hold on anymore," I said to Cori between gasps as I swam back to the boat. I couldn't last any longer either. The fresh air felt like a million pinpricks deep inside my lungs but it also felt good, like soothing aloe vera on a sunburn.

"Holy crab cakes. That really is a tail." Cori crouched over the side of the boat and got her first good look at me sporting fins. "That is the freakiest thing I've ever seen. Can I touch it?"

"Have at it," I said between gulps. "But don't get too close. I've been known to puke."

Cori ran her hand along my tail, which was now prickling with heat. I held onto the side of the boat and searched the water to see if I could spot Serena or Luke. As much as I wished I could just dive into the water to find them, it was too late. I was changing back.

Finally, after what seemed like forever, Serena appeared with Luke in her arms. I put my hand to his chest. Unconscious but still breathing. I turned to Cori.

"My grandmother's cottage is just up ahead. We need to get him there." I tried to ignore the searing pain coming from my tail, but I could tell it had already begun to split. It burned like ten thousand hair straighteners.

Serena, can you carry Luke to the boat shed? I rang to her and pointed to my Gran's about a hundred yards away. She nodded.

"What can I do?" Cori asked, looking desperate.

I took a deep breath, relieved that the pain in my legs was subsiding, but for once, the thought of legs didn't fill me with its usual glee.

"Pass me my shorts?"

Trey bumped the boat against the dock, and Cori and I jumped out to tie it off to Gran's dock. A quick look up at the cottage showed an empty driveway, which was good since it meant Gran wasn't home but bad since Dad hadn't arrived with the Merlin 3000 yet. Cori had called and told him where to meet us. I needed a way to keep Luke safe and hidden in the meantime. I remembered how I'd kept Mom in the rowboat full of water inside the boat shed. No one would see him in there. Why reinvent the wheel?

"Meet you in the boat shed." I pointed and found the boat shed's key under the rubber mat. Trey jumped in the water to help Serena with Luke. Once inside, I opened the garage door to let them in, then pressed the boat-lift button to lower the rowboat down from the rafters.

Trey held onto Luke in the chest-deep water.

"Where's Serena?" I asked.

"She took off toward that island back there." Trey pointed to the Becker's cottage.

"Why would she do that?" I wondered out loud as I climbed into the rowboat, now settled in the lake. I pulled the plug to let the water in.

"Maybe to steal another dog?" Trey joked but his face was tense and his hands shook. "So, what do we do now?"

"Wait a sec until I can get this thing flooded, then we can pull him inside." I helped the process along by dumping water into the boat from the lake with the plastic bailer.

Cori buzzed around the boat shed, looking jumpy and wound up. "What can I do? Give me something to do!"

I remembered how Mom had felt so much better after I'd added bath salts to the lake water, although Luke didn't seem like the spa type.

"Can you run up to my grandmother's cottage? Get the box of salt from the cupboard above the microwave. The key is under the garden gnome by the door."

"I'm on it," Cori said before disappearing out the door.

"Best to keep that girl busy. How is he doing?" I asked,

turning to Trey. The rowboat was now three quarters full and I searched underwater to plug the hole.

"Not good."

I reached out to grab Luke's arms underwater. "Here, help me get him in here."

It took a little maneuvering to keep from tipping over, but Trey helped keep the boat steady as I pulled Luke over the stern.

"What do we do now?" Trey said once Luke was safely inside the boatful of water.

"Well, hopefully my dad got the Merlin 3000 working again. Then everyone can get back on their own two feet."

Karma is a crazy thing because just as the words left my mouth, Trey's arms flew up and he stumbled back into the water.

"Trey! Are you okay?" I jumped onto the boat shed's side dock and pressed the button to raise the rowboat out of the way so Trey could get his balance. But Trey hadn't lost his footing. Something had him. Something hairy-armed and ugly.

Finalin! I rang through the air, hoping the sound made it through the water to him. The splashing stopped and the bubbles cleared so I could see him properly. It was the same scruffy pockmarked face, now filled with hate and betrayal. He held Trey around the waist, leaving him to sputter for breath at the water's surface.

Where is she? Where is my daughter? Finalin screeched.

I don't know! She was with us but she left. I considered

jumping in to help Trey but what if Medora was lurking just outside the boat shed door? She could pull me under as well. Then what would happen to Luke?

Just let him go! I pleaded.

No! Make Serena a Webbed One. I know you can. Then I let go. He pulled Trey under again as I watched in horror. Trey flailed underwater, struggling for air.

"Okay, okay!" I yelled, forgetting my mermaid voice. *I can do it. I'll do it!*

Finally, Finalin let Trey resurface. He coughed and gasped for breath.

Just then, Serena swam into the boat shed.

No.

Finalin glanced from Serena to me. *Yes, Serena. This is your chance. Your chance to be free.*

No! Serena said more forcefully. *You made me leave home once before, but I belong here with you, with mother.* She held out her hand and motioned past the frame of the garage door. Medora swam into view and drifted to her daughter's side.

You betray me? After all we've sacrificed? Finalin screeched. His face flamed red and he tightened his grip on Trey. *I will not have it. My daughter will not suffer as we've suffered.*

Finalin looked at me fiercely and pulled Trey under again. This time I couldn't help it. I ran around the narrow dock skirting the inside of the boathouse and launched myself into the air, cannonballing into the water behind him. Who did this guy think he was?

Hélène Boudreau

I said, let go of him!

I grasped onto Finalin in a piggyback and pulled at his arms, his hair, anything I could to get him to let go of Trey. Finalin thrashed and bucked like a wrestling crocodile, forcing me underwater. The back of my throat burned with the rush of lake water flooding my nostrils, setting off a big red panic button in my brain. What had I done? Did I really think I could take on a fully grown mer-maniac?

All of a sudden, I heard a *WHACK* and Finalin's body went limp. I let go and grabbed onto Trey to help him to his feet as Medora and Serena swam to Finalin's side.

"Whoa! What the heck?" Trey stood and caught his breath, then scrambled onto the dock. "That guy is crazy!"

"Not as crazy as I am." Cori stepped out of the shadows, brandishing an oar and a smug look.

"Nice shot!" I held out my hands for Cori and Trey to help me onto the dock before Medora decided I should take Trey's place. But Medora didn't look like she was out to get anyone. Finalin's eyes fluttered a bit and Medora looked back at me with a slight smile. She whispered something to Serena, then disappeared out the boat shed door with Finalin in tow.

Sorry about that. I crouched down on the dock while Cori and Trey poured the box of salt into the rowboat and checked on Luke.

Don't worry. He has a hard head. Serena turned to where Medora had just disappeared, then smiled at me. *Tshank shoe,* she said in English.

No, thank you. *But are you sure about this? About staying here, I mean?* I asked. *The rest of the mer-world considers Talisman Lake a prison, you know.*

A prison, yes, but home for me. Serena scanned the lake and nodded. *For now.*

Okay, but if you ever change your mind about this... I checked to make sure Medora and Finalin weren't nearby and felt for the chain around my neck with the toe ring pendant. Perfect. I hopped back into the water and waded over to Serena, then placed the chain around her neck as she held her long hair out of the way. *This will be our signal.*

Serena looked up at me through the water and held the toe ring between two fingers. I searched around the boathouse dock and spotted a loose metal spike from one of the spars. *Hang it from there. I mean, if ever you want to become human again.*

Serena nodded and dropped the pendant to her chest. Then she swam to the lake's bottom and found a sharp rock and looked like she was cutting long strands of her hair.

What are you doing? I asked, horrified.

She ignored me and weaved her hair into an intricate rope-like braid, then swam back to me and tied the braid around my wrist like a bracelet.

Like a friendship bracelet. I remembered making something similar during summer camp.

Friend. Serena touched my arm, then looked up at Trey and Cori before turning tail and disappearing out of the boathouse and into the lake.

Just then, Eddie and Dad stumbled into the boathouse. Dad's hair looked like he'd been through a wind tunnel and his glasses were perched precariously at the tip of his nose.

"Sorry it took so long! We had to go to three computer stores and the traffic to Dundee was nuts. There are some *really* crazy people out there!"

"Dad," I said, grasping his hand to climb out of the water one final time, "you have *no* idea."

Chapter Twenty-Two

T HE GOOD NEWS WAS that we got Luke safely installed in the trailer without attracting the attention of the neighbors. The bad news, though? The computer still wasn't hooked up, so the Merlin 3000 was no better than the flooded rowboat in Gran's boat shed.

Eddie rode in the trailer with Luke to try to get the computer working while Cori, Trey, and I piled into the car with Dad.

"How long before it's working again?" I asked as we zoomed along the roads of Port Toulouse.

"Eddie needs to reload the data and recalibrate the settings, but Jade..." Dad rubbed a hand over his scruffy, unshaven face.

"But what?" I asked, holding my head. "Please don't give me any more bad news."

"We just have to remember that the Merlin 3000 is an unproven prototypical experiment based on theoretical extrapolation," Dad said.

"English, please?" I begged.

"It's just that it's never been tested in the field before," Dad replied. "Even if we get it operational, there are no guarantees it will actually work."

"Lalalalala." I put my fingers in my ears and sang to block out his voice. I knew it was childish but I couldn't stand to listen to another word. The Merlin 3000 *had* to work. Then life could finally get back to normal again.

Dad pulled onto our street at top speed and narrowly missed a long black sedan parked along the road.

"Whoa." I braced my hand against the dashboard and hoped Luke hadn't splashed out of the Merlin 3000 in the back of the trailer. I looked back toward the official-looking car we'd almost rear-ended and couldn't help thinking it looked about as out of place as a penguin in a chicken coop. "Who are those guys?"

Dad looked in his rearview mirror and frowned. "They were parked there earlier this morning too."

Trey and Cori glanced over their shoulders as well, then we all turned quickly when one of the guys in the car with horn rimmed glasses looked up from his newspaper.

"Do you think they're watching us?" A fist-sized lump grew in my throat. "Could they know something?"

Dad exhaled a noisy breath and checked his mirror again. "I'm not sure, but it's best if we keep cool." He glanced at Trey and Cori. "Cori, would you mind heading home? The fewer people hanging around the better."

"Sure," Cori replied.

"And Trey, I see your parents are here, so act like you've

been invited for a barbecue or something." Mrs. Martin had been discharged from the hospital and their car was parked next to our driveway.

"No sweat," Trey replied.

"Jade," Dad backed up the trailer into our open garage, "you go inside and check on Mom."

A familiar panic rose inside me. Mom and Luke were finally back on land, but I was starting to realize our lives as mers would never be anywhere close to normal.

Trey helped Dad unhitch the trailer while his parents joined them at the garage. They all stepped inside and shut the garage door.

I glanced up the street to the sedan and caught the driver with the mustache looking at me. "Text me when you get home?" I asked Cori.

"You're trembling," she said, grasping my arm. "Are you going to be okay?"

I took a long, shaky breath and nodded to the garage. "Depends what's happening in there."

"Don't worry, it'll all work out," Cori said quietly. "Your dad is the smartest guy I know. Call me if there's news, okay?" She waved as she headed down the street.

I waved back and headed up the front steps to the house. Sure, Dad was a genius when it came to things like calculating the density of air, but I couldn't help worrying that the Merlin 3000 would be a replay of the bathroom faucet fiasco.

I swung open the front door to rush inside and check

on Mom, but got a text from Bridget reminding me about my split shift at six (darn!) and tripped over a pair of orthopedic shoes with familiar *Bet Your Bottom Dollar* laces, which sent me sprawling in the front hall.

It was true. Friends shouldn't let friends walk and text.

"Smoly Hokes! Jadie, honey, what's your hurry, sunshine?" Strong hands grasped me to help me up.

"Gran!" Gran was here. Mom was here. A mer-boy was floating in a hot tub in my garage. Gah!

"What are you doing here?" I blurted—maybe a bit too loudly and a touch too forcefully.

"Don't get your flip-flops in a twist. Can't an old lady drop in and visit her favorite granddaughter?" Gran answered. But there was a twinkle in her eye. "Plus, I had to swing by the bank in town to cash my check from the big bingo jackpot the other night."

Gran reached into her handbag on the hall table and held out an envelope full of cash.

Gran *had* won. Big time! But what was I doing just standing here? Luke could be fighting for his life in the garage! And what about Mom? Where was she?

"What's the matter, Jadie girl? You look like someone just stole your Popsicle."

Gran could read me like a poker hand, but I couldn't exactly tell her what had me so freaked out.

"I, uh, I'm just really in a hurry to get to work." I found a hair elastic in a dish on the hall table and scraped my hair into what I hoped looked like a ponytail. "Plus, it doesn't help that I have to do my shift at the ice cream parlor with Chelse Becker. That girl doesn't know the difference between strawberry and chocolate sauce."

"Isn't she the Beckers' daughter with the cottage up my way? I thought she spent her summers there."

"She usually does, but she had to take a job to pay her parents back for a canoe they think she lost but—" I stopped before I revealed too much. But back to the task at hand: mer-Mom, mer-boy, mer-ME, Gran. I had to get Gran out of there.

"Don't worry. I know all about the canoe." Gran looked at me with an understanding look on her face.

"You do?" I asked.

Just then, Mom stepped out from the kitchen holding a mug of steaming tea. Her hair was cropped short in a blond pixie cut.

"Yes, indeed." Gran looked from Mom to me and smiled. "In fact, your *Tanti Natasha* told me all about your little canoe trip across Talisman Lake."

"Oh! Tanti Natasha." I crossed the hall and put an arm around Mom, plastering a smile on my face. "So, you've met?"

"We most certainly have." Mom kissed the top of my head.

Gran slapped her thigh and chuckle-snorted. "Oh, Jadie! You should see the look on your face."

"So, you know all about how Tanti Natasha is from Tonganesia? And about her daughter Serena..." Oh, I'd have to revise my story now that Serena was out of the picture. "Who just went back to the old country to go to boarding school?"

Mom gave me a wide-eyed look.

I'll fill you in later, I rang to her.

Gran played with the setting on her hearing aid, probably wondering if that's where she'd heard the ringing. "Yes, yes. I know all about Serena and about your boyfriend in the hot tub in the garage and those maniacs who pulled your mother underwater that awful day last summer."

She knew. She knew everything.

"You're not freaked out, are you?"

"Jadie, honey." Gran laughed. "I've been to Las Vegas seventeen times. It takes a lot more than a couple of mermaids to freak me out."

"Gran even cut my hair." Mom patted her new hairdo and flashed me a smile.

Cori's mom also stepped out from the kitchen. Mrs. Blake and Mom had been best friends since they met at a Stroller Striders walking club when Cori and I were in diapers. She held an empty box of hair dye.

"We had a bit of a spa day," Mrs. Blake joked.

"Speaking of hair, Jadie"—Gran pointed to my lopsided, poker-sticky ponytail—"have you looked in a mirror lately?"

I rushed upstairs to get brushed and changed, then headed to the garage to check on Luke before I had to get to work in seventeen minutes.

"How is he?" I hurried down the short flight of stairs into the garage from the rec room.

"We're getting him stabilized." Dad had taken the soft top off the trailer, and he and Eddie were busy adjusting the settings on the Merlin 3000 while the Martins watched nearby.

Mrs. Martin sat in a lawn chair near the trailer looking pale and tired, mostly from her recent trip to the hospital, I imagined, but it probably didn't help that her son was in a state of mer-suspension at that moment. I handed her Luke's phone from my backpack upstairs.

"I hope you're feeling better?"

She smiled and patted my arm. "Yes, thank you."

"How's everything going? Is it working?" I turned to Dad.

"The computer is back online and we're recalibrating the sensors." He stepped down the trailer steps to let me in. Eddie sat at the counter, monitoring graphs and numbers on the three computer screens in front of him. He waved and returned to the conversation he was having via videoconference as he worked.

My vision adjusted to the low light from the lone bulb lighting the garage. Luke's eyes were still closed.

"But he's still unconscious?" I turned to Dad.

"Yeah." Dad grimaced and rubbed his hand over his hair. "We're trying to figure that one out. His pulse is elevated, but otherwise he looks okay. Eddie's speaking with Bobby in Florida, and she says there's a comatose period for mers when they go through the change."

Bobby was a *she*? I looked past Eddie's shoulder and

sure enough, a woman about Eddie's age smiled back at him. Our eyes met and she waved.

"Luke told me his best time was two days." I leaned heavily against the side of the Merlin 3000. "Is it going to take that long with this thing?"

"Well." Dad squeezed by me to go check a graph on the computer screen. He adjusted one of the leads attached to a probe submerged underwater. "If my calculations are correct, it should actually speed things up, because normal tides work on a six-hour cycle and ours is optimized to two. We might have him back on two feet later today if all goes well."

"And if it doesn't work?" I asked.

Dad looked over at the Martins and took a deep breath before answering.

"Luke's parents have decided to give it twenty-four hours, but if there is no measurable transformation, we'll have to transport him back to the ocean. Kind of a catch-and-release effort, if you will."

"You can't do that!" I exclaimed. "You didn't see those Mermish Council guys. You've heard how protective they are of the Webbed Ones secret. Who knows what they'll do to him if they catch him again?"

"Let's not get ahead of ourselves," Dad said quietly.

Gran had opened the door to the garage and was standing at the top of the stairs.

"Hey, Jadie, sweetie?" she called over. "Don't you need to get to Bridget's?"

"No." I couldn't just leave Luke there. What if he woke up? Or worst of all, what if he didn't wake up? "I'll call Bridget and tell her I'm sick or something."

"Jade—" Dad began.

"You're not seriously going to make me go to work with all that's happening, are you?" I asked in disbelief.

But by the look on Dad's face, I knew the answer. He pulled me into a hug. "There's really nothing else you can do here. We'll call you the second there's any kind of news. Deal?"

"Fine." I stared down into the tub and hoped Dad and Eddie knew what they were doing. Otherwise, Luke may never become human again.

Gran jingled her eight ball key chain from her purse.

"Well, pitter-patter and I'll drive you over there. Besides, I'm stacked full of bills and have a real hankering for an ice-cold treat."

Chapter Twenty-Three

C HELSE GOT GRAN'S ICE cream order ready while
I went to the kitchen to get ready for my shift.
I laughed out loud when I saw the piled up ice cream,
smushed bananas, and pool of chocolate sludge.

Gran looked up at me with a bewildered expression
from her seat at the counter.

"See what I mean?" I whispered. "But until I can come
up with another seventeen weeks' worth of paychecks to
pay for the rare aboriginal canoe I lost, she's here for the
long haul."

Gran ate a spoonful of ice cream and considered this for
a moment.

"Chelse, honey? Can you come over here for a sec?"
Gran called Chelse over from her perch on the stool by the
cash register.

To her credit, Chelse put her phone away and walked
over sweetly. "Anything else I can get you, Mrs. Baxter?"

"Oh, no thank you. You've done a tremendous job on
this…" Gran looked at her dish.

"Banana split?" Chelse offered.

"Yes, yes," Gran continued, "banana split. But there's something I've been meaning to tell you. You know that old canoe of yours?"

"Yes?" Chelse answered.

I stood behind Chelse and shook my head to keep Gran from blowing my cover. She continued anyway.

"Well, I feel really bad but one night—" Oh no! Gran was about to take the blame for the canoe. I couldn't let her do that. Or could I? Chelse wouldn't get mad at a sweet old grandmother, would she? *My* sweet old grandmother.

"I did it!" I blurted. Chelse and Gran both turned to look at me. I cringed, thinking of how I'd let Chelse work there all summer when I really should have confessed from the very beginning.

"Jade," Gran began, but I held up my hand to stop her.

"One night," I continued where Gran left off, trying to be as truthful as possible, "when Gran was out, I took your canoe for a ride, but it tipped over and I had to swim to shore. I'm really sorry, but it was dark and I lost your canoe."

"And"—Gran looked at me with a knowing glance— "I'm partly to blame because Jade was staying with me and I'd left her unsupervised. So I want you to take this for your troubles." She fished into her handbag and slid a familiar-looking envelope of money across the linoleum counter. Chelse picked it up and looked inside. Her eyes grew wide.

"Wow, I don't know what to say."

"Just promise me," Gran rested her hand on Chelse's and eyed her seriously, "that you'll give up any aspirations for a career in the dairy industry?"

"Thank you!" Chelse smiled widely and returned to the counter to get back to her texting.

"Gran!" I hushed. "You didn't need to do that. I would have paid her off eventually."

"Oh, you're not getting off that easily. You still owe me for half so keep scooping, Jadie girl." Gran winked and fastened her handbag, then stood up from her stool. "Now, gimme a kiss."

She leaned over the counter and gave me a sweet peck on the cheek.

"Do you want to take that to go?" I pointed to her disaster of a banana split.

"Of course! No need to waste it." Gran slid the takeout box I'd handed her underneath her dish and took a generous bite, waving her spoon in the air as she headed for the door.

"Are you mad?" I asked Chelse once the traffic at the ice cream parlor window finally died down at about 7:30. She hadn't said a word to me since Gran left.

Chelse looked up from her phone. "Not exactly mad. More curious. Why didn't you say something when I first got here? We could have worked something out."

"I guess I was kind of scared of what you'd think of

me," I said as I cleaned the counter with a damp cloth. I couldn't exactly tell her I'd stolen the canoe to rescue my mermaid mother, but I definitely owed her an apology. "I'm sorry. And really sorry you got stuck working with me all summer."

Chelse picked up a dish towel to help me dry the counter. "It hasn't been all that bad. We got to hang out, plus I've learned a few new tricks of the trade."

"Yeah, um, your banana split is really coming along," I offered.

"I was thinking more of my dish towel ninja skills." An evil grin crossed Chelse's face as she twirled her towel and snapped it toward me in a perfect Cori-inspired flick.

"Nice!" I dodged her shot and laughed. "I guess I deserved that."

"Call it even, then?" Chelse tossed the towel over her shoulder.

"That depends," I said. "Are you gonna keep flicking me with that thing?"

Chelse smiled mischievously as she continued her texting. "You just never know when the ninja dish towel will strike," she joked.

"Okay, I guess I deserve that too." I laughed "Thanks, Chelse."

I checked my phone too. There was a text from Cori saying she'd made it home okay and one from Lainey Chamberlain wondering if I'd found the Environmental Assessment yet.

"Oh darn." I muttered. I sent a text to Dad to see if he could grab it from the pocket of my jean shorts and bring it to me when he came to pick me up after my shift.

"Anything wrong?" Chelse asked.

"No, nothing serious," I replied, though I could easily come up with about a dozen things that were actually wrong at that very moment. Then Lainey's text reminded me of something. "Hey, did you get the Facebook invitation to the big beach party?"

"Yeah." Chelse smiled. "But I think I've had enough of Facebook for one summer." She tucked a strand of hair behind her ear as she studied the screen of her phone. A familiar bracelet hung from her wrist. I looked down at my own wrist to the bracelet Serena had given me.

"Chelse," I said slowly. "Where did you get that bracelet?"

Chelse looked down at her wrist and her lips grew into a sad smile. "Oh. A friend of mine made it for me when we were kids."

I covered my bracelet with my hand, not knowing if I should show it to her. Then an idea grew in my head. Chelse had said a few weeks before that she wasn't the only one who could be hurt by the video on Facebook. I pulled out my phone and checked Facebook, remembering that Chelse had edited out the part where she'd fallen in the water in the version she'd made. Was there something in that part of the video she didn't want others to see?

After clicking through a few links, I finally found the

original video her ex-boyfriend had posted and played the last few seconds. I followed Chelse's gaze to something she'd spotted in the water, impossible to see unless you were looking for it. But there it was; the unmistakable outline of a shimmering mermaid's tail.

"Her name is Serena," I murmured, looking up.

"Huh?" Chelse asked.

I placed my phone on the counter. "Your friend. The one who's trying to save you from drowning in the video. The one who gave you that bracelet. Like the one she gave me. Her name is Serena."

I held up my wrist to show her my bracelet made from Serena's hair.

Chelse's hand was over her mouth and her eyes glassed over with tears. "How—I haven't seen her all summer. I looked for her everywhere and then my mom and dad made me work here and I was afraid—"

That's why Serena disappeared toward the Becker's cottage when we got to Gran's. She was looking for Chelse too.

"She's okay. And she's back," I said.

"I've known her since we were kids," Chelse said between tears. "Every summer she'd come. I kept her secret."

I stared down at my bracelet, then looked around to make sure no one was around.

"I have an idea," I said quietly. "I think you should take that envelope of cash my grandma gave you and pay your parents back, then enjoy the rest of your summer up at your cottage. Leave the ice cream scooping to Cori and me."

"But what about my shifts?"

Bridget emerged from the kitchen just then, catching the tail end of our conversation.

"I think that's a great idea!" Bridget had done her share of covering for Chelse's scooping deficiencies. She actually looked a bit relieved. "There are only a few more weeks left in the summer. I think with a bit of juggling, Cori, Jade, and I can cover the ice cream parlor."

"Thanks, Bridget!" Chelse hugged her.

"Not a problem, hon." Bridget crossed the diner and turned off the neon open sign. "In fact, you ladies can start cleaning up because we're closing up early."

"Really? Why?" I asked.

"Got that big catering gig from Chamberlain Construction. I've got enough people to man the barbecue grills for the beach party, but I'll need your help getting the buns and burgers down there. After that, consider your-selves off-duty."

Just then, I got a text from Dad.

@geeksrule: all is well but nothing new to report. lainey (?) called. found the paper, told her I would bring it to you at beach party. xo dad

I guess I was going to the beach party after all. Given the way things seemed to be working out, maybe it would be a good distraction. Plus, I owed it to the Butterfly vs. Boutiques people to at least show up, after they'd been so awesome at the rally.

I clicked back to the Facebook invitation and pressed *accept*.

Chapter Twenty-Four

THE TOULOUSE POINT BEACH parking lot was completely full, and cars were parking up along the canal's concrete pier by the time we finished unloading all the burgers and buns from Bridget's van.

Chelse headed back to her parents' cottage in Dundee and Bridget was busy with the barbecues, so I strolled down to the boardwalk, hoping to spot someone I knew. A huge bonfire sent glinty sparkles dancing into the evening air while a band played music from a nearby bandstand for the gathering crowds.

Apparently, news of Chamberlain Construction's beach party had spread through Facebook after all, and Port Toulousians were easily won over by the promise of food and free, live music.

"Jade!" I turned to see Cori walking toward me.

"Hey!" I wrapped her in a hug, relieved to see a friendly face. "You're here!"

"On my first *date*," Cori said with a sheepish grin.

"Your mom is finally letting you date?" I asked.

"Well, I promised you'd be with me and there'd be a group of us, but yeah. Except, Trey's not even here yet, which makes this the *lamest* first date ever." Cori looked around the crowd, trying to spot him. "He must still be at your place. Have you heard anything?"

"No," I replied. "I got a text from my dad a while ago, but nothing since. I just hope everything works out okay."

"It will." Cori put an arm around my shoulders and walked along the boardwalk with me. "Besides, I'm counting on your underwater connections to launch my new mer-inspired fashion line. I think I'll call it 'Knee-High Fashions.'"

"Ah, Cori." I laughed out loud. "You're awesome. You know that?"

"So I've been told." Cori squeezed my shoulder.

"Jade! Oh, Jade!" My whole body stiffened at the sound of the voice calling for me from behind. I turned and plastered a smile on my face.

"Lainey, hey!" I called out, then turned to Cori. "Darn. She's going to ask me for that Environmental Assessment and I still didn't get it from my dad," I whispered.

"Why is she so bent on getting that thing from you, anyway?" Cori asked.

"I have no idea," I replied.

Lainey Chamberlain strutted down the boardwalk toward us in her too-high sandals, toting Cedric in her oversized handbag.

My phone buzzed with a text. It was Dad. He was in the parking lot waiting for me.

"I know, I know." I held up my hand to stop Lainey from asking for the obvious. "My dad has the papers for me in the parking lot. Hold on here and I'll go get them—"

"No," Lainey interrupted. "Daddy has been bugging me to get that thing from you all day. I'll come with you."

But what if Dad had Mom with him? Sure, Gran and Cori's mom had done her hair and she looked way different, but I really didn't feel like explaining a brand new woman in my dad's company to Lainey. Cori caught my drift when I flashed her a bug-eyed look and she cut in.

"Lainey," Cori exclaimed, "I just love your sandals. Did you get those in New York?"

Lainey brightened and turned her foot from side to side to display her sandal in all its glory. "Actually, yes."

"I keep meaning to ask you about your trip," Cori continued. "Which designers did you and your mom go see?"

Cori took Lainey by the shoulders and steered her toward the bandstand.

"But," Lainey said, looking over her shoulder. But by then Cori had complimented her on her bag too, giving me enough time to make my getaway to the parking lot.

I spotted Dad's car and weaved through the rows of cars to meet him. Mom was in the passenger seat, wearing a baseball cap and sunglasses. She rolled down her window.

"Hi, sweetie," Mom said.

"I'm not sure it was such a good idea to come here." Dad glanced around the parking lot, looking nervous.

Mom put a hand over his. "Don't worry, Dal. I'm

home, we're all safe, and that's all that matters. Nobody can do anything to us now." She turned to me and took my hand too.

A warm feeling spread through me, knowing that Mom was always going to be there for me now, no matter what. She was right. We'd worked too hard to make her human again; there was no way anyone or anything was going to ruin that.

"Wait. Who's home looking after Luke? Is everything okay?" I asked.

Mom snuck a peek at Dad then turned to me and smiled. "More than okay."

I put a hand to my mouth. "It worked? The Merlin 3000 actually worked?"

"Better than we expected," Dad chimed in. "And I didn't even have to call Mr. Zooter!"

"Where is he? Where's Luke?" I looked around to see if I could spot him.

"He came with his parents," Mom said. "Which brings us back to our conversation from earlier. Your dad and I have been talking about you dating."

"Oh! Is that a hot dog stand?" Dad said. "Jade, you stay here with your mom. I'm just going to go grab us a couple hot dogs for the road."

"Bye, Dad." The car door slammed.

"Coward." Mom laughed and turned to me. "So, Luke, huh?"

"Yeah." I felt the heat rise in my cheeks, remembering

our embarrassing almost-kiss on the rocks below the construction site. "Except, I'm pretty sure I already messed up my chances with him."

"You never know until you ask," Mom said with a smile.

"You mean, you're saying it's okay for me to date?" I asked.

"Yes. But with a group—just as long as you're with Cori too."

I had a feeling the Baxters, Blakes, and Martins all had some sort of dating protocol conference call. Still, though.

"I dunno—" My phone buzzed. Another text from Lainey. "Oh! Did you guys bring that Environmental Assessment thing?"

"I gave it to Luke," Dad said as he returned with the hot dogs.

"Okay, cool." I glanced around to make sure no one was looking and gave Mom a peck on the cheek. "Thanks. And you too, Dad."

"My pf-leasure," Dad said between mouthfuls of hot dog. He put the car in drive and began to pull away. "Pf-ick you up at t-fen!"

The car pulled away in a cloud of dust. When it cleared, another car came into view. It was the same black sedan we'd seen on our street earlier with the mustached driver and the guy with the horn-rimmed glasses. My breath caught short and my palms began to sweat. What did those guys want? Did they know our mer secret? Were they trying to expose us?

I ducked behind a minivan before the sedan guys could see me, dashed back toward the bandstand, and texted Dad to warn him to watch out for their car. A huge crowd had gathered, making it hard to get around, but I saw Cori and Lainey standing at the other end of the stage.

Once I sent the text to Dad, I took a deep breath and scrolled through my contacts until I found Luke's number. *Fluke1019.* He answered on the second ring.

"Hey, Luke?" I asked.

"Jade."

"I'm *so* glad you're okay, and that the Merlin 3000 actually worked."

"Your dad's a pretty smart guy," Luke said. "He's thinking of changing goldfish into ferrets next. Could be a whole new business in it for him and my grandpa."

We both laughed at the same time and then the phone line went awkwardly quiet.

"Oh hey, do you have those Environmental Assessment papers for me?" I asked. "Lainey is breathing down my neck for them."

"Yeah, I've got it here—" Luke's voice was cut off by the musicians on the bandstand striking up, like some kind of celebration was about to start.

Chamberlain Construction banners graced the top of the stage and the band music died down as Mr. Chamberlain walked up to the microphone. A series of chairs were lined up to his right and a collection of local dignitaries, including the mayor and a group of women and men in business suits, were sitting in them.

"Welcome, everyone," Mr. Chamberlain said. "Welcome!"

Mr. Chamberlain's pinheads clapped and grinned like idiots, trying to encourage the audience to join in. There was a small round of applause.

"Thank you, thank you very much," Mr. Chamberlain continued. "Thanks to the unrelenting support of Mayor Miller and his council, and the citizens of Port Toulouse, Chamberlain Construction has been bringing green buildings to this community for twenty-five wonderful years."

More pinhead applause.

"Lately, my engineers have been hard at work," Mr. Chamberlain continued, "designing innovative ways to protect precious green spaces while giving you the shopping experience you deserve. Today, I am thrilled to announce the *re*imagined design for the Port Toulouse Mall renovation."

One of Mr. Chamberlain's pinheads pulled a cloth off a large poster propped up on an easel. It was the same construction design spanning the back of the mall over the tidal pool, only now they'd added a walking path and what looked like container gardens.

"Are you still there?" I asked Luke over the blare of the band striking up another song.

"Yeah," Luke said. I could hear the shuffling of papers on the other end of the line. "Hey, that's weird."

"What?" I asked. "Where are you, anyway?"

"I'm by the lifeguard tower," Luke said. More rustling paper sounded through the phone. "I'm sending you a picture."

A text pinged on my phone and I opened the attachment. It was a picture of the design plan for the mall construction from the Environmental Assessment, but it looked nothing like the poster up on stage.

"This isn't the same design," I said into the phone. The wing on the Environmental Assessment followed the highway. It was nowhere close to the tidal pool.

I hunted through the crowd to see if I could spot the lifeguard tower, but the sun was setting and it was getting hard to see. Finally, I saw Luke and tried to catch his eye, but he was busy taking a picture of something else on the paper.

Just then, I got a text back from Dad.

@geeksrule: nobody following us. are you sure it was the same car? xo dad

That's when I saw horn-rimmed glasses and mustache guy. And they were standing right behind Luke!

"Luke, watch out! Behind you!" I called into the phone. Luke put the phone to his ear and looked around. "What?"

But before I could warn him further, the mustache guy snatched the Environmental Assessment out of Luke's hand and made a beeline for the stage.

"What? Who was that guy?" I could see Luke twist his head around, trying to figure out what had just happened.

"They've been hanging around our street all day," I replied. "Now I know why."

Lainey Chamberlain perked up at the other end of the stage, catching on to what had just happened. She got her father's attention at the podium and pointed toward the mustache guy holding the paper as he waited in the wings. Then she hugged Cedric and smiled.

The Environmental Assessment. Those mysterious black sedan dudes weren't after us, trying to uncover our mer secret. They were working for crooked Mr. Chamberlain, trying to cover up a construction scandal. And given that Lainey had been hounding me for that Environmental Assessment all day, I had a feeling Cedric was a bit of a payment for all her hard work.

"That Environmental Assessment is a fake," I said into the phone to Luke. "That's why those guys have been tailing us."

While the band played on, Mr. Chamberlain walked to the wing of the stage and took the papers from the guy with the mustache. He glanced at the Environmental Assessment and smiled smugly, then folded it and tucked it inside the breast pocket of his blazer before walking back out to the podium. He signaled a thumbs-up to the mayor, then whispered something to the same pinheaded minion who tried to snatch the Environmental Assessment from me the day before. The pinhead held up his hands for the band to stop playing so Mr. Chamberlain could continue speaking at the microphone.

"So, to conclude, thank you so much for coming

everyone! Enjoy the food and drink and entertainment. It is my pleasure to have you all as my guests," Mr. Chamberlain said. "The future looks bright for Port Toulouse Mall, and we will stop at nothing to bring you the Green Shopping Experience you deserve!"

The crowd must have bought into what he was saying, or maybe they were under the influence of too much barbecue sauce, because a few cheered and clapped as Mr. Chamberlain and his pinhead posse linked hands and raised them in the air like a football team that had just won their final game.

"How do they think they're going to get away with building a mall with a fake Environmental Assessment?"

"Look at the other text I sent you," Luke replied.

I checked my phone, and sure enough, there was another text with an attachment. This time it was a picture of a handwritten note at the bottom of one of the pages.

Dear Martin,

You won't be able to pass an environmental assessment with the new plan we talked about, but go ahead with construction anyway and use this assessment in its place. I'll make sure it gets pushed through the Land Development Department no questions asked. That should cover up everything.

Pleasure doing business with you! Looking forward to our next round of golf.

Frank Miller

"That's a note from the mayor!" I gasped.

"I guess we know how Mr. Chamberlain plans to get away with it, huh?" Luke asked.

I glanced up at the stage as Mr. Chamberlain and Mr. Miller and his council shook hands and patted each other on the back. It reminded me of the Mermish Council pushing Luke around and laughing about the fact that they'd framed Finalin and Medora for a murder they didn't commit.

A seething anger roiled up inside of me. Mr. Chamberlain had almost killed my mom and Serena with his truckloads of dirt. Then he'd laughed at us when we had tried to take a stand for the Monarch butterfly.

"Hey!" I yelled over the music from the band. I rushed toward the stage, fumbling with my phone as I tried to forward the photos to a place where I knew they would make difference. I stumbled up the stairs of the stage as I went, but I didn't care. There was no way these guys were going to get away with their plan this time.

"Hey!" I yelled even louder as I crossed the stage to the podium where the mayor and Mr. Chamberlain stood smiling and laughing. I grabbed the microphone. It squealed in my hand, making everyone look up. A few kids put their hands to their ears.

Mr. Chamberlain looked my way and didn't recognize me at first.

"I have a feeling," my voice cracked as I looked at him, then I turned to the crowd, "that you may want to rethink your plans for the Port Toulouse Mall."

"Oh really?" Mr. Chamberlain asked with a bemused look on his face.

"Really," I replied. I found Luke in the crowd again. He was standing with Cori and Trey while Lainey untangled herself from the crowd and stalked up the other stairwell at the far end of the stage.

"What do you think you're doing?" she cried as she hurried toward me.

"Just explaining to the wonderful people of Port Toulouse that your daddy and Mr. Mayor here have been building an illegal mall extension without a proper Environmental Assessment."

"You have no proof of that," Mr. Chamberlain muttered through gritted teeth. "Not anymore," he whispered so only I could hear and patted the breast pocket of his blazer.

"Oh really?" I turned to the crowd. "Mr. Chamberlain here doesn't think we have any proof that his Environmental Assessment is a fake. How many of you out there are from the Butterflies versus Boutiques Facebook page?"

A round of applause filled the night air, causing a wide grin to cross my face.

"Then," I continued, trying to speak loudly and clearly in the microphone so everyone could hear, "would you all be so kind as to check out the page and let me know if we actually *do* have proof?"

A murmur rippled through the crowd as people fumbled through their pockets and purses for their phones. Then one by one, once they found the pictures I'd hurriedly posted on the Butterflies vs. Boutiques page as I stumbled up the stage's stairs, they held their lit-up phone screens in the air. It was only a few at first, then dozens, but soon hundreds of glowing cell phones dotted the darkened beach. The beginnings of a chant began to form.

"Green means green! Butterflies not Boutiques!"

"Green means green! Butterflies not Boutiques!"

By then, Lainey had found the pictures on Facebook too and was holding up the screen for her father to see.

"Daddy!" she cried. "That's why you wanted me to get that paper for you? Well, then you can take Cedric back!" She held out her bag, then reconsidered when Cedric whined for her. "Well, no. You can't have him back, but now I want a *horse*."

Mr. Chamberlain looked from me to Lainey, to the audience, then to the mayor, and gulped.

Good thing his helicopter was waiting nearby; otherwise, I'm not sure he would have made it off the beach alive.

Chapter Twenty-Five

HUNDREDS OF PEOPLE CAME up to me afterward to thank me and congratulate me for finally putting a stop to the mall construction. I was mostly on the edge of tears the whole time, overwhelmed by everyone's support. Little did they know that saving that part of the coast not only helped the Monarch butterfly, but eventually, when the tides cleared the muddy waters away, mers who needed the tidal pool would be able to use it to become human.

The crowds finally thinned out as people spread out along the beach to enjoy the warm summer evening.

Cori spread her beach blanket onto the sand and dumped her stuff. "We're going to get a couple hot dogs to celebrate. The works?"

"Yeah, thanks," I said.

"What about Luke?" she asked.

"I dunno. I kind of lost track of him." I bobbed my head up and over the crowds to see if I could spot him.

"I think he went to get something from the car," Trey said.

"Just call him on his cell," Cori suggested as they headed for the barbecues.

"Good idea," I replied as I watched them go. But all of a sudden I felt unsure again. Yes, Luke was back and Mom was back and life was normal again—as normal as it was going to be, anyway. But what did that mean for him and me? Were we friends? More than friends? I had to know. I took a deep breath and dialed his number.

"Hey, Luke?" I said when he answered.

"Hi," he replied. "Sorry I haven't had a chance to talk to you yet, but you were really awesome up there."

"Thanks to you!" I paused before continuing. "Listen, Luke. I was wondering…" I left the sentence hanging, not knowing what exactly I was wondering. Wondering if he'd like to hang out? Vague. Go out on a date? Lame. Be my boyfriend? Scary.

Whatever the question is, the answer is yes. I heard the ring coming from over my right shoulder.

Luke. I looked over and spotted him by the lifeguard tower again, holding his phone to his ear. His guitar strap was slung across his chest.

"Will you guys *stop* with the squealing and hang out like two normal people already?" Cori returned with an armful of hot dogs while Trey carried the drinks. She nudged me and winked as they laid the food out on a blanket.

When he saw I'd noticed him, Luke slipped his phone into his pocket and smiled—that curvy-lipped adorable smile that turned my legs to jelly. Was I ready for this?

Ready to take the next step? Who knew? Maybe I wasn't ready to jump in with two feet, but would it hurt if I just dipped in a toe?

I was going to ask you if you'd finally play that guitar for me, I said, walking toward him.

I dunno. My concerts usually sell out. There may not be any tickets left. Luke held out his hand for me as I approached.

Darn, I replied. *I was hoping for front row seats.*

Luke took my hand in both of his and held it to his chest.

"I'm *so* glad you're back," I whispered.

"Glad to be back," he replied. "I kinda missed you."

I took a deep breath and drank in the salty ocean air, then took a leap of faith...and kissed him.

Was Luke my dream guy? My soul mate? My boyfriend? Only time would tell. But right then, the moment, the guy, the kiss—it all felt right.

"So, about that concert," Luke whispered in my ear, "would you settle for a seat on a piece of old driftwood overlooking a puddle?"

"That, my friend"—I took his hand and led him toward the point—"sounds absolutely perfect."

Cori's 5-Minute Lunch Bag Chocolate Popcorn

―

Snacks at sleepovers are a must.
Try this one next time your parents
forget to stock the snack cupboard.

Supplies:

   brown paper lunch bag

   stapler

   measuring cup

   microwave

Ingredients:

¼ cup	popcorn kernels
2 tbsp	brown sugar
2 tbsp	chocolate chips
2 tbsp	butter or margarine
	pinch of salt

Pour the popcorn kernels into a brown paper lunch bag then fold the top of the bag ¼ of an inch, twice. Secure two staples (trust me, I Googled it!) at the folded part to seal the bag shut. Lay the bag flat in the microwave and cook on HIGH for about 1:45 (one minute and forty-five seconds, people!). Each microwave is different, though, so you may need to adjust the time.

Meanwhile, add the brown sugar, chocolate chips, butter/margarine and salt to a microwave-safe measuring cup. Cook on HIGH for about 15 seconds or until the gooey buttery-chocolaty mixture is melted. Mix well with a fork then pour it over the popcorn.

Toss like a salad and ENJOY!

You. Are. Welcome.
:) Cori

Acknowledgments

Writing a book is a lot like making an enormous ice cream sundae but it is a process made much easier with a drizzle of keen-eyed critique pals, a sprinkle of super-patient friends, and a big glob of family.

Much thanks to my agent, Lauren MacLeod, who scooped me out of her slush pile and kept me from going nuts through all of my writerly efforts. Thanks also to my editor, Aubrey Poole, who never waffled and provided the cone of truth I needed to tell this story as genuinely as possible.

Marcelle, Charlotte, and Gord: you are the cherries on top of everything and my constant sources of support and inspiration. None of this happens without you.

About the Author

Hélène Boudreau never spotted a real mermaid while growing up on an island surrounded by the Atlantic Ocean, but she believes mermaids are just as plausible as giant squids, flying fish, or electric eels. She now writes fiction and nonfiction for kids from her landlocked home in Ontario, Canada. Her first book of this series, *Real Mermaids Don't Wear Toe Rings*, was a 2011 SCBWI Crystal Kite Award finalist.

You can visit her at www.heleneboudreau.com.